Contents

Kiran Doshi is a retired diplomat and educationist. His novel *Jinnah Often Came to Our House* won The Hindu Prize in 2016, and his short story 'Miss Coelho, English Teacher' was shortlisted for the 2019 Commonwealth Prize. His other works include *Birds of Passage*, a novel, and *Diplomatic Tales*, a work of comic fiction written in verse.

He lives in Delhi.

The ENGLISH TEACHER

and other stories

KIRAN DOSHI

SPEAKING TIGER

SPEAKING TIGER BOOKS LLP
4381/4, Ansari Road, Daryaganj
New Delhi 110002

Published by Speaking Tiger Books in paperback 2021

ISBN: 978-93-90477-11-1
eISBN: 978-93-90477-19-7

10 9 8 7 6 5 4 3 2 1

Typeset in Electra LT Std by SÜRYA, New Delhi
Printed at Chaman Enterprises, New Delhi

Author's Note

All the stories in this collection feature women, ranging from the ages of three to eighty—women I have known, met or learnt about from friends. The stories feature some men, too, but as extras. The punchlines belong to the heroines. The stories are based on true events—some more than others, and one, 'Cherchez la femme', almost entirely—but, I hasten to add, in the form that they appear in these pages, they are all works of fiction.

Do the stories answer that old, old question that has troubled men since Adam: What are women really like? Perhaps they do. They certainly answered the question for me, as I wrote them: Women are like men, only different, mostly better.

The English Teacher

A couple of days after Miss Coelho got the Best Teacher award, the following Letter to the Editor appeared in the *Times of India*, Mumbai edition.

The 10th of September

Dear sir/madam,

I have just seen the photograph in the Times of India of Miss Coelho receiving the Best Teacher award.

Better late than never, I suppose. But the Government could have given her this award twenty, thirty or even forty years ago, when she became a teacher; for even then, in fact on her first day at work, she was the best. She knew better English than anybody else, was eager to teach it and, best of all, knew how to teach it—be it to a class of thirty or to a single, lost child, like I was. She mesmerized us with her eyes, her voice, her sudden smiles, her wit, her pointing finger, her frowns, her praises, her pauses, her other teaching tricks...all of them designed to make every lesson a sort of game for us, often leaving us breathless. She never bothered to consult any textbook or notes, and whenever she used the blackboard, did so with the speed of lightning, as if she was afraid of wasting any of the precious moments of the forty-five minutes allotted for the period... She never missed a class. Nor did we. Yes, she gave us homework, but always homework that helped us to climb a rung or two more of the long ladder to good English. And yes, she gave us tests, plenty of them, but not to grade us, and certainly not to pass or fail us. She gave us those to find out where she *had failed* us, *so that she could take the necessary corrective steps. Almost every evening she stayed back late to help children who needed special care. She still does, I am sure. Not one of us—her girls—failed to do well in the Class X and XII board exams, and later, to pursue careers of our choice. If St Patrick's is today the best girls' school in the whole of Colaba and perhaps in the whole of Mumbai, it is almost entirely because it has her on its staff.*

She will turn sixty next year. I hope that the powers that be will not let her retire then. She is worth her weight in gold. She will be horrified to read this letter, I am sure. For she is a very private person. But I had to write it, I just had to.

Mrinal Deshpande
Zee TV

It is not known if Miss Coelho read the letter. Probably not. She considered newspapers a waste of time. As for the powers that be, it did not matter what the letter said. Rules were rules. Miss Coelho had to go the day she turned sixty and the slot vacated by her had to be given to someone from a weaker section of society.

~

Retirement held no terror for Miss Coelho. Fr De Souza had already offered her something purposeful to do—editing *The Call of Jesus*, the journal of the church. True, it was a quarterly, so the work would not occupy much of her time, perhaps no more than a few hours every week, but it was something she was sure she would like to do. For years now, while attending the Sunday mass, and recalling how Lord Jesus had come to her aid in every moment of crisis in her life, she had prayed for a chance to serve Him. Now, at last, she had got her chance... And maybe, by and by, she might be able to prevail upon Fr De Souza to expand the scope of the journal to include in it a section on good English! It was shocking the way even educated people wrote English these days.

As for the other terror of retirement, how to meet her daily expenses, she did not have to worry about that either! Following her dear father's advice, she had religiously saved fifteen per cent of her salary every month, rain or shine, for almost forty years, and invested it in fixed deposits of the Bank of India, as solid a bank as any. The interest from those alone should be enough to meet all her expenses, leaving the capital intact for emergencies. Why, she might even be able to go on a trip to Jerusalem someday, something she had always wanted to do! In the meantime, she could afford a few luxuries, couldn't she? She bought herself a slice of bebinca from Fonseca's on the way home.

~

Home was a high-ceilinged, first floor flat in an old, double-storeyed house in Gulmohar Lane, a cul-de-sac off Colaba Causeway. Crowded when her grandparents and parents were still alive, and her sister Carmina not yet married, the flat was now almost too large for her alone, consisting as it did of a large living room ending in a wide wooden balcony on the street side and flanked by a bedroom, a study, a bathroom and a kitchen on its left. The best part of the flat was its rent, Rs 75 per month, thanks to the Rent Control Act, which did not allow owners of old houses to increase rents. Fortunately, her landlord, a nice, kindly man not much older than her, but one always in poor health, had never pestered her to vacate the flat, like some other landlords in Colaba. Nor, after his death some six months back, had his wife or son, although she ran into them frequently since they lived right below her, in the ground floor flat of the house.

~

Her part-time help, Shantabai, had already arrived when she reached home, and, between chores, gave her news of the day, as she did every evening. The price of onions had gone up again; the Government was doing nothing about it… Minister Bhonsle, the one who was always making speeches on closing down dance bars, had been caught visiting a brothel; men were like that only… Babaji (Miss Coelho's landlord's son) was migrating to Australia…

A long time back Miss Coelho had stopped questioning the news Shantabai brought her. But what she had just said was so unexpected that she could not help asking, 'Are you sure? He might be planning only to visit Australia. How do you know that he is migrating to the place?'

'Everybody says so,' Shantabai said by way of reply. 'His mother is staying on,' she added, completing the news. She had more news to offer and she continued, 'The bus stop for number 106 is being shifted; it will be on the other side of the post office now… There was a shootout between Pahadi Pehelwan's gang and some smugglers near Sassoon Docks last night; one of the smugglers was killed…'

But Miss Coelho was not listening; she had turned pensive. The young man's departure for Australia would be the end of an era. The families had known each other since 1944, when her grandfather, moving from Goa to wartime Bombay to take up a job in Defence Accounts, had rented the flat and lived in it to the ripe old age of eighty-two. The family had celebrated his eightieth birthday with a party, inviting, among others, the landlord and his family. Ah, those were happy days, filled with people. Now both the first and the ground floors of the house would have just one woman each.

After dinner, perhaps because of the sombre mood that Shantabai's news had put her in, she pulled out her box of memories from below her bed and went through its contents: handmade greeting cards from past students; a thin silver chain with a crucifix that had belonged to her grandmother once; her Best Teacher award; her passport, never used and long expired; counterfoils of the tickets to

Dr Zhivago, which she had seen with dear Desmond on their first date; her only photograph with him, with both of them sitting close, one behind the other, on a made-up crescent of a moon in a Flora Fountain studio; the band of gold she had worn for six months; the yellowed, last letter from him, written three days before he had finally succumbed to cancer.

She knew every word of the letter. She read it again nevertheless. It wrenched her heart as it had every time she had read it in the…thirty-nine years, two months and five days.

Darling Maria,

I don't mind dying, except that I wanted to prove my father wrong. He used to say that marriage is the graveyard of love. I know that our love would only have increased with every passing day, year after year.

Can you do me one last favour, darling? Don't become a nun. Continue teaching. You are a fantastic teacher. And teaching too is serving Our Lord.

Yours, as ever,
Desmond

Dear Desmond. How she used to long for his voice, so deep, so caressing; and those dimples that formed on his cheeks every time he smiled; and the sweetness of his breath every time he came close… Lying in bed that May evening, amid the falling shadows of his Tata Cancer Hospital ward, he had returned to her the engagement ring on his finger and asked her to get married to someone nice after his death. Fighting back tears, she had slid the ring back on his finger, given him a smile and asked him not to talk nonsense; he was going to be all right… He had died an hour later. She had wept for days after that. When she had stopped at last, it was with a sudden realization that she was never going to weep again, for she was never going to be able to love again… There was no question of her marrying after that. But, following his other advice, she had continued teaching and, through that, learnt to live with his loss. Could Desmond have given her the advice for that reason, to help her bear the loss? Wait a minute. Could Lord Jesus have given it—thorough Desmond, of course? That was how He worked, through others. Yes, that must have been it.

~

Her prayer before sleep that night was longer than it was most nights, but she slept fitfully, and woke up the next morning with an inexplicable sense of loss. Retirement blues? She got out of bed briskly to shake off the blues and made herself a cup of tea. What was it that she had planned to do this morning? Yes, to go to David Sassoon Library and borrow *Usage and Abusage, a Guide to Good English* by Eric Partridge, which, the library had written to her, was now available. Then, at eleven-thirty, she was meeting Fr De Souza at the church. On the way back from church, she was going to buy some groceries.

Just as she was leaving for the library, however, the postman came with a letter for her. It was from her bank, conveying that three of her fixed deposits were maturing on the first of the next month and would be automatically rerolled for a further period of five years… A routine letter. She was about to fold it back when a sentence at the bottom of the sheet caught her eye: *Following the lowering of the repo rate by the RBI, new rates of interest will apply to fresh deposits.*

What did it mean? That she would get less interest? Surely not. Her FDs were not new. They were old; they were only being rerolled. But then why that sentence in a letter to her? She went to the bank.

The bank manager liked Miss Coelho. His daughter had studied at St Patrick's and was now an assistant manager in HDFC. He ordered tea for her, explained to her the complexities of high finance and at last answered her question: the new, lower rate of interest—six and a half per cent, as against the previous seven and a half per cent—*would* apply to her FDs.

'Even though mine are really old FDs?' she repeated.

'I'm afraid so, Miss Coelho. You see…' And he repeated what he had already told her.

'All that I can say,' she murmured after hearing him out once more, 'is that lowering interest rates like this is most unfair to people who have retired and therefore have only their savings to live on.'

'I know,' he murmured. 'I wish I could help.'

'Never mind,' she murmured and rose to leave. 'Lord Jesus will find a way.'

'Ye-s,' he mumbled, rising. 'Yes, of course.' And suddenly he added, 'Why don't you give tuitions, Miss Coelho? Now that you have retired, no one can stop you from giving tuitions. And there is a crying need for good tutors of English. Why, just the other day my assistant manager told me that he is looking for a tutor to help his son…'

That is how Miss Coelho started giving tuitions, beginning with the son of the assistant manager of her bank. Before the month was out, she had three more pupils. She taught them for an hour every day, Tuesday to Saturday—and individually, which she believed was the best way to teach, for every child had its own speed of learning. On Sundays she attended mass, edited *The Call of Jesus* and sometimes visited her sister in Bandra. Mondays she spent on personal work, read books, and prepared lessons for the next week, not that she really needed to prepare for them. She knew her job—imparting to the pupils all the four linguistic skills: understanding, speaking, reading and writing. She also knew what parts of grammar she needed to teach them to impart the skills, and in what order: nouns, determiners, verbs, pronouns, basic sentence structures, adjectives, predicates, adverbs, conjunctions, interjections, complex sentence structures, punctuation marks, direct and indirect speech, phrases, clauses, similes, metaphors, idioms, proverbs… And she knew what pitfalls Indian students faced when learning English.

Inevitably, her fame spread. She was not just the best tutor in the whole of Colaba but also, bafflingly, the most affordable, a bargain really. Before six more months were out, she was giving tuitions to seven children of various ages—oddly, all of them boys—and had no space for any more.

'Maybe you should charge your pupils a little more,'

the bank manager suggested to her when she went to the bank one Monday. 'Seven hundred rupees a month per child—that too for individual tuitions—is far too little these days.'

'I'm not giving the tuitions to become a millionaire,' she said tartly, 'but only to make good the loss from your lowering—so unfairly—the interest on my FDs.'

Old ladies!

'It was beyond my control,' he protested and mollified her with the usual cup of tea and praise for what she had done for the English of his assistant manager's son. 'I'm so glad,' he smiled and said at one point, 'that you accepted my suggestion and decided to give tuitions.'

'That is vanity,' she admonished, wagging a finger at him. 'It was our Lord Jesus who made the suggestion through you.'

~

The next evening, when her last student had left and Shantabai had just served her a cup of tea, the door opened—it was never locked in daytime—and a man she had never seen before entered the flat, closed the door behind him and stared at her.

'Yes?' she said, raising an eyebrow.

'Are you the teacher?' he asked, darting his eyes to Shantabai and back.

'Y-es...'

'Come with me,' he said, taking a step forward and holding out his hand.

'I beg your pardon!'

'Pahadi Pehelwan wants to talk to you.'

She heard Shantabai gasp and turned to see her hand covering her mouth, her eyes wide in alarm. She turned back to the stranger and said, 'If this Paha... If he wants to talk to me, ask him to come here and talk to me.'

'Didn't you hear me?' the man cried, his voice raised. 'It is Pahadi Pehelwan who wants to talk to you.'

'There is no need to raise your voice,' she said, her voice unchanged. 'I can hear very well.'

The man made to take another step forward but checked himself, took a deep breath, turned round and stormed out of the flat, leaving the door open.

'Why are you behaving like a frightened rabbit?' Miss Coelho cried to Shantabai when she could not hear the sound of his steps any longer. 'Do you know that man? And for heaven's sake, come out of the kitchen.'

Shantabai stepped out of the kitchen. Beads of perspiration covered her brow.

'Do you know the man?' Miss Coelho repeated. Shantabai shook her head.

'Hmm,' Miss Coelho frowned. 'Who is Pahadi Pehelwan?'

'The...the...Raja of Colaba.'

'Raja?' Miss Coelho cried. 'What do you mean, Raja?'

It took Miss Coelho many questions to learn that it was Pahadi Pehelwan, not the police, nor the Municipal Corporation, and certainly not the Government, that ruled Colaba. Maybe nice people like her did not know that, but everybody else did. Pahadi Pehelwan did not deal in drugs or prostitution, but dealt in everything else. Probably half of the shop-owners of Colaba paid hafta, weekly tributes, to him.

'Why?' Miss Coelho was puzzled.

'*Why*, memsahib?' Shantabai wet her lips.

'Yes. Why?'

'Because…things happen to people who don't do what he says,' Shantabai murmured, giving the open door a quick glance.

'I see,' Miss Coelho digested the information. 'So why does he want to meet me?'

That stumped Shantabai. 'I don't know, memsahib,' she said in the end. 'But I don't like it, that man coming here. I hope he does not come again.'

'He will,' Miss Coelho said. 'He has gone to his master for orders on what to do next. And the next time he comes, don't behave like a rabbit. Face him like a man.'

~

Miss Coelho was right; Pahadi Pehelwan's man had gone back for orders on what to do next. In his whole life, Pistol—yes, that was the name by which the boys knew him—had never been so surprised as that evening. The old woman had actually refused to obey Pahadi Pehelwan's summons. Should he have just picked her up and carried her to him? Maybe he should have. He had almost done that. Something in the look she gave him had stopped him. Now he did not know what to say to the boss.

To his relief, Pahadi Pehelwan did not explode when he told him what had happened. He only stroked his chin. 'Very well,' he said at last. 'Let us go and meet her.'

And so it happened that just when Shantabai was beginning to breathe normally again, Pahadi Pehelwan, closely followed by Pistol, walked into the flat.

Miss Coelho was still seated at the table, a spoon in hand, a bowl of tomato soup before her. Pahadi Pehelwan stared at her for a moment. She stared back at him.

He was the first to speak. 'I've come to ask you to teach my daughter English.'

She put down the spoon. 'I cannot take any more pupils. My days are full.'

'You won't have to teach her much—only enough to pass the entrance test of St Patrick's School.'

'Only!' she cried. 'Only! Do you know that the entrance test of St Patrick's is the most...'

'And not for long,' he continued, 'only three months.'

'I... What do you mean, only three months?'

'Peri—that's her name—is already five years old. She has to pass the test this year.'

'And you are coming to me today! You want me to teach her in three months what takes—'

He put up a hand. 'It was not my idea to put her in St Patrick's. It was my wife's. I promised her the day she died that I would put her there.'

'Still, you could have...' Miss Coelho checked herself. 'When did she die?'

'Last Saturday. She had cancer.'

Miss Coelho stared at him for a long time without saying anything. 'Where is Peri?' she asked in a murmur when she spoke again.

'At home. I did not bring her with me because I don't

like to see her disappointed. I mean, in case you said no. She is all that I have now.'

Was that a glint of tears in his eyes? Miss Coelho looked away.

'How much English does she know?' she asked when she looked at him again.

'Not much, I think. She can sing "Twinkle, Twinkle, Little Star". My wife had hired a teacher…'

Miss Coelho sighed. That was all the English that teachers seemed to be teaching children these days: 'Twinkle, Twinkle, Little Star'. And maybe 'Baa, Baa, Black Sheep'. 'I'll need to teach her for an hour and a half every day, five to six-thirty, Monday to Saturday,' she said at last.

'Thank you. My car will pick you up at a quarter to five tomorrow.'

'My pupils come to my place,' she said evenly.

He hesitated, turned to look at Pistol, looked back at her, opened his mouth to say something but changed his mind. 'All right,' he said. 'I'll bring her here before five tomorrow.' He brought out a wallet from his pocket and proceeded to pull out notes from it. 'Your fees…'

'I don't charge fees in advance,' she said.

'I just thought that, er…maybe a little…'

'I'll let you know how much at the end of the three months.'

~

Miss Coelho was prepared to be kind to the girl whom cancer had robbed of love, and who entered through her door the next afternoon, holding her father's hand, with large, unblinking eyes that stared at her uncertainly. What she was not prepared for was what happened next: she fell in love with the girl. It happened suddenly, when the girl edged closer and gave her a hesitant smile, bringing out dimples on her cheeks. For a few seconds she could not utter a word... The girl was the daughter that she and Desmond would have had. She wanted to hug the girl, cover her with kisses, tell her that everything was going to be all right...

'What is your name?' she asked her instead.

'How old are you?' she asked her next.

'Read the words on this page,' she said next.

The girl knew none of the words. She barely recognized the letters of the alphabet.

'Every afternoon from five to six-thirty,' Miss Coelho reminded Pahadi Pehelwan when he returned to pick up the girl, 'Monday to Saturday.' She added, '*And* on Monday morning from eight to ten.' She knew that she would need every minute of those hours to prepare the girl for the test. She also knew that all of a sudden she wanted nothing more in life than to help the girl do well in the test.

~

To her delight, the girl turned out to be a good learner. Before the first month was out, she could grasp almost everything that she said to her, so long as she spoke slowly and used only the words and sentence structures that the girl had learnt already. She could speak small sentences herself—happily without making any grammatical mistakes. And she had a functional vocabulary of almost three hundred words. But she had still a long way to go, Miss Coelho knew. Her vocabulary had to be enlarged. Her irregular verbs and prepositions had to be strengthened. Her reading aloud had to be made smoother. Her writing skill had to be developed...

~

One evening, when she was teaching Peri similes, Shantabai dropped a bombshell. 'Babaji has come from Australia for a few days,' she said. 'He is selling the house.'

'What!' Miss Coelho was astonished. 'Why?'

'He is buying a house in Australia.'

'What about his mother?' Miss Coelho asked. 'Is she too moving to Australia?'

'No. She is moving to an old people's home in Vashi.'

Miss Coelho was too shocked to ask any more questions. Shantabai went on nevertheless.

'Someone called Manwani is buying the house. Nobody in Colaba knows anything about him. He is from Chembur.'

~

A week later the new owner of the house paid her a visit.

'I believe you are a busy person, madam, so I'll come straight to the point,' he said. 'I want you to vacate this flat. I'll pay you one lakh rupees for that, plus your moving expenses. You can go to Goa, or to your sister in Bandra, or an old people's home, it doesn't matter where.'

'I've no wish to live elsewhere,' she said.

'Two lakhs,' he said.

'I was born here...'

'Five lakhs.'

'...and I've lived here all my life,' she said.

He gave her a long, hard look and said, 'That's my final offer. Please think it over.' And he left.

~

'Manwani is a builder,' Shantabai told her that evening. 'He wants to pull down the house and construct a big building here, with shops and everything.'

'He can't do that,' Miss Coelho said. 'The Rent Control Act forbids it. It is precisely to protect tenants from unscrupulous builders like him that the Government has made the law.'

'People say that he has the Municipal Commissioner in his pocket,' Shantabai said.

'Even the Municipal Commissioner can't do anything against the Act,' Miss Coelho said. 'Only Lord Jesus can,' she added, remembering her dear father's joke, 'and He is on the side of the poor!'

She dismissed Manwani from her thoughts. She had no time to waste on him anyway. She had to complete the editing of the articles, poems, letters, thoughts...and other tidbits to be included in the forthcoming edition of *The Call of Jesus*. Moreover, three of her pupils, apart from Peri, had to appear for important tests or examinations in the next few months. Peri herself had reached the point from where, if guided with care, she could make rapid progress.

~

One day, when she was explaining irregular verbs to her, the girl said, out of the blue, 'My papa says that mummy has gone to God.'

'That's right, Peri.'

'Radha says she is dead.'

'Who is Radha?'

'My best friend. She says mummy will never come back.'

'When people die, Peri, they go to God, who lives in heaven. They don't come back but they watch us from there. They never stop loving us.'

'Will mummy always love me?'

'Yes. Always.'

'I will also always love her. And papa… And also you too,' she added suddenly.

Miss Coelho looked away and cleared her throat. When she spoke again, it was to say, 'We can't use *also* as well as *too* in the same sentence, Peri. We can say "*also* you" or "you *too*", never "also you too".'

~

Manwani paid her his next visit a few days later, when she was in the midst of teaching Peri how to write letters in the cursive script, always a difficult task.

'I can increase the amount to seven lakhs,' he said without any preliminaries.

'I told you I'm not interested in leaving this place,' she said.

'That is my final offer,' he said. 'I would advise you to accept it.'

'What do you mean, advise me?' she asked.

'You will regret not accepting it,' he said.

It was a threat, she realized, but an empty threat, she felt. The law was on her side. And she really had no time for empty threats. Peri's entrance test was just two weeks away. Moreover, Fr De Souza had reminded her that the final proofs of *The Call of Jesus* had to be submitted to the printers by the tenth of the next month. She had assured him that she would complete the editing well before the date, though the English of the contributors to the journal really left a lot to be desired, she had added. Maybe the journal should start a section on good English; she would be happy to handle the section. He had frowned and said that it was *what* the writers said, not *how* they said it, that mattered. Not giving up, she had pointed out that some of the things that the contributors were trying to convey were written in such terrible English that they made no sense; surely, the contributors would serve Our Lord better if they wrote more intelligibly. And thus they had argued for full fifteen minutes, till finally he had said—absurdly, she felt—'Let us not forget, Miss Coelho, that Our Lord Jesus too did not know good English. And yet he could deliver the Sermon on the Mount.'

~

The weeks passed in an instant. At the end of the period, Miss Coelho was reasonably confident that she had prepared Peri for the test, but for the first time in her life, she was nervous. One never knew with entrance tests. On the last day of the tuition, she conducted a mock interview of Peri. Did she do well enough in it? She was not sure. Almost five hundred girls would be appearing for the entrance test this year, she had found out. Only thirty-five would be selected. Peri did not have to merely pass the test, she had to pass it with distinction.

That evening, when Pahadi Pehelwan came to collect the girl, he brought out his wallet and asked her to name her fees.

'I will have to calculate the amount,' she said. 'Come and meet me on Monday evening.'

'Monday morning is Peri's test,' he reminded her.

'Yes. Come after the test.'

The next day was Sunday, the day of mass. Miss Coelho stayed on in church after the mass, praying, and walked back in deep thought. Mr Manwani was waiting for her below the house along with the ward officer for Colaba from the Municipal Corporation, come there 'to examine the stability of the building'. Surprised, for there was nothing wrong with the building, she let them into her flat nevertheless. The man spent ten minutes in it, examining walls and making notes in a little book he was carrying.

That evening Shantabai told her that Manwani had asked the Corporation to declare the building unsafe. That would let him evict her and raze the building.

Miss Coelho closed her eyes, as if in prayer. 'Lord Jesus will take care of us,' she said when she opened them.

~

She spent Monday afternoon in her chair with a book, looking up at the door from time to time. Five o'clock. Six o'clock. The door opened but only to let in Shantabai. Miss Coelho continued sitting, sipping tea. Seven o'clock. Seven fifteen… The door burst open when she had almost given up hope, and an exuberant Pahadi Pehelwan, carrying a shyly smiling Peri, rushed in with the news. 'Peri has been selected! She stood first, along with two other children. All three got exactly the same marks.' He put down the girl.

'I am very proud of you, Peri,' Miss Coelho said, giving her a smile. The girl beamed back at her, bringing out her dimples in all their magical allure. From far away Miss Coelho heard Pahadi Pehelwan ask her, 'Your fees, madam. Name your figure—any figure.'

She looked at him.

'I'm the happiest man in the world today,' he said.

'Two thousand and one hundred rupees,' she said. 'That's my fee.'

'What nonsense!' he cried. 'I'm giving you one lakh.' He put a bundle on her table.

'You will take that right back,' she said. '*I* decide what I charge my pupils.'

The battle lasted many minutes this time. As usual, she won it.

'But isn't there anything else that I can do for you?' he asked.

'There is nothing, thank you,' she said. 'I've everything I want.'

'There must be something,' he persisted.

'There is nothing,' she repeated.

He shook his head, took Peri by the hand, and went out of the door. She moved to the window and from behind the curtain watched them cross the street and get into a car. Peri turned to look up before getting into the car, and her heart skipped a beat. But the girl looked away without waving and got into the car… She must not have been visible behind the curtain, she realized. By the time she pulled the curtain aside, the car was gone. She moved back into the room and asked Shantabai to make her another cup of tea. She did not want anything to eat, she said. Shantabai stared at her for a moment, stunned to see tears where she had never seen them before, and went into the kitchen to make her tomato soup and toast, determined to force her to eat those at least.

~

'There must be something that the woman wants,' Pahadi Pehelwan said to Pistol the next morning. 'Nobody in the world wants nothing.'

'Yes, boss,' Pistol nodded. 'Nobody wants nothing.'

'She is a strange woman,' Pahadi Pehelwan mused some more.

Pistol waited.

'Ask that bai of hers,' Pahadi Pehelwan said in the end. 'She would know. There must be something that the woman wants.'

~

So it happened that the next evening, when Miss Coelho was sipping tea, the door of her flat burst open and somebody rushed in and fell prostrate before her feet.

'What on earth…' she cried and tried to move her feet away.

It was no use. Two large hands had clutched them, sandals and all. A face, pausing only to cry 'Please forgive me', had buried itself on them and, horror of horrors, was now proceeding to kiss the sandals.

'Shantabai!' she called out. 'SHANTABAI!'

Shantabai rushed out but stopped when she saw the man.

'It is that Manwani fellow,' she said, folding her arms.

'Manwani?' Miss Coelho stared at her uncomprehendingly and looked down to verify.

'Please forgive me,' his voice came up muffled from between her feet. 'I had no idea that you knew such a mahan purush, such a great man.'

'What are you talking about, Mr Manwani?' she cried. 'What is he talking about, Shantabai?' She looked up at Shantabai helplessly… 'Please leave my feet, Mr Manwani!' She looked down again.

'First say you forgive me,' he said.

'Oh, this is ridiculous! Please get up Mr Manwani.'

'No,' he said. 'First forgive me.'

She tried to pull away her feet. A string of a sandal broke.

'LEAVE MY FEET!' she cried.

'First forgive me,' he repeated.

'GET UP.'

'Forgive me.'

'Oh God…' she looked at the ceiling for help.

It was Shantabai who broke the logjam, 'If you ask me, memsahib, forgive him and let him say what he wants to say.'

'Eh? All right. All right. I forgive you,' Miss Coelho said. 'Now please get up.'

It took him some moments to scramble to his feet and join his palms in supplication. Beads of perspiration ran down his head.

'Stay in this flat as long as you like,' he said. 'I don't want you to vacate the flat. In fact, I insist that you stay on. And don't pay me any rent. Yes, I don't want any rent. And please go on the pilgrimage to Jerusalem. *I* will pay for the ticket. I will pay for all the expenses too. There is an excellent group tour next month…'

~

'Well… That was a surprise,' Miss Coelho said to Shantabai after Manwani had left them at last. 'Who do you think caused the change in his heart?'

'Who, memsahib?'

'Our Lord Jesus, who else? Remember? I told you, He would take care of us.'

'Yes, memsahib,' Shantabai nodded, but with a smile.

'But this tea has gone cold,' Miss Coelho said. 'You would not mind warming it up, would you?'

Before the tea could be warmed, there was a knock on the door. It was Fr De Souza. 'I was passing this way,' he explained, as Miss Coelho rose from her chair, 'and thought maybe I should drop by and tell you that I have given further thought to your suggestion. Maybe we *should* introduce a column in *The Call of Jesus* on the importance of good English. I mean, the English of some of our contributors does leave a lot to be desired…'

'I know, I know,' Shantabai said after he had left, and before Miss Coelho could say anything, 'It was Lord Jesus who spoke through him.'

~

As for her going to Jerusalem, she had to postpone the trip. A few days before she was scheduled to leave for it, Pahadi Pehelwan went to her and asked her if she would continue teaching Peri English—till the end of the first academic year.

'Where is Peri?' she asked, excitement surging in her heart.

'Downstairs in the car,' he said, 'I didn't bring her up because I don't like to see her disappointed. I mean, in case you said no...'

Saga-vhala

The Gujarati word for relatives is *saga-vhala*. *Saga* means related; *vhala* means loved or dear ones. Literally, therefore, *saga-vhala* means related-loved. Wags say that the word is an oxymoron. How can anyone related to you also be dear to you? Meet a relative after ten years and the first thing he says is: 'You did not offer me even a cup of tea when I came to your house the last time.' Half of the battles fought in the villages of India are between saga-vhalas. Not just in the villages, in the cities too.

Take the case of Asha, my sister.

She was born in Churchgate, south Bombay, did her BA from Jai Hind College, south Bombay, and married a boy from Marine Drive, south Bombay. You can't get more urban than that. By the way, her marrying a boy from south Bombay was not a coincidence. It was her condition for getting married. 'I will marry only someone from south Bombay,' she had said to everybody—grandmother, father, mother, uncles, aunts, cousins—since she was probably in primary school. South Bombay, for her, was—it still is—a clearly defined territory: any place south of an arc drawn from Haji Ali to Bhindi Bazaar to the Docks, and where only vegetarians live. Every place north of the line is a no-go place, even to visit. In all her life, she has gone north of the arc on only three occasions, each time to Bandra, and always to watch the shooting of films featuring Amitabh Bachchan, to which she had been specially invited for winning quiz contests on Bollywood films.

She is crazy about Amitabh Bachchan. She is crazy about films, period. She sees a film a day, rain or shine, and often more than one film a day. She must have seen well over ten thousand films in her life so far, including films with titles such as *Chandni Chowk to China* and *Padmashree Laloo Prasad Yadav*. (Yes, there are films like that.)

Mostly, however, she sees classics, films like *Awara*, and *Chaudhvin ka Chand*, and *Anand* and… 'Our best films were made in the black-and-white era,' she likes to say. 'They have a magic that no film made in colour can ever capture.' That does not mean that she does not see modern films. She has seen *Bajrangi Bhaijan* five times, *Kuch Kuch Hota Hai* nine times, *Sholay*, her all-time favourite, fifteen times. But whenever she sees a film made in colour, she turns off the colour knob on her TV and sees it in black and white. We don't challenge her when she does that, remembering that she is an expert, but if you ask me, few things in life are more horrible than seeing, say, *Sholay* in black and white.

Vasant, her husband, is four years older than her, therefore almost six years older than me, but I know him as well as I would my own brother. He is the answer to every girl's prayer for a good husband. He does not smoke, does not drink, does not play cards (even without stakes), never looks at a passing woman… I am a hundred per cent sure that he has never violated any commandment of any religion, let alone of us Jains. In fact, he also observes a long list of what I can only call homemade commandments. He never reads a newspaper at the breakfast table; always eats whatever my sister dishes out to him; always wears whatever clothes she buys for him; goes to office straight from home; returns home straight from office; never leaves his shoes here and there; never asks her for the remote of the TV; never forgets to put back the seat of the toilet; never opens his mouth when she is shouting at the children, or the housemaid, or at him...and always hands over to her his pay cheque on the first of every month.

My grandmother says that his father was also like him, bhagwan no manas, a saint, therefore, alas, without a spine or the life skills that a man needs in a place like Bombay. About the only manly thing that the old man ever did was to rent a flat in the Sea Vista building on Marine Drive after the old tenement building in which he was living in Kalbadevi had suddenly collapsed in the heavy rains of 1976. That year, it may be recalled, was the year of the great Emergency in India. Flats to rent were available for a song in Bombay. His cost him Rs 350 per month. True, it was an inside flat, so for a vista of the sea about fifteen feet wide, he had to put his head out of the kitchen window and turn it sideways. But it had three bedrooms, a rare luxury. Moreover, thanks to the Rent Control Act of Maharashtra; its rent could never be increased, even after he died. The flat became Vasant's mother's when he died and Vasant's when the mother too passed away some years after Vasant and Asha got married.

~

It was an arranged marriage. He, his mother, and his mother's brother (who had travelled all the way from Rajkot for the purpose) had come to our place, taken a good look at Asha, sitting quietly on a sofa across, eaten the khaman dhokla and rasgullas that my parents assured them had been made by Asha, sipped tea (which *had* been made by her) and left. Two hours later, probably following a family talk, his mother had called to say that they were agreeable to the match. They did not ask for any dowry (because, we learnt later, Vasant did not approve of dowries). We had celebrated the day by eating up the rest of the rasgullas.

'How does he look?' Asha asked me after the last of the rasgullas was gone and we were alone.

'Who?'

'He. Who else?'

'Didn't you take a good look at him?'

'Don't be an idiot. How does he look?'

'Like a cinema star,' I quipped.

'Really?... Which star?'

'Amitabh Bachchan.'

'Really?' Her eyes lit up.

'Well, he is tall,' I mumbled, retreating carefully.

'Hmm. Tall is not all,' she mused, then suddenly burst out, 'Stupid rules our community has. One can't even see one's husband before marrying him. One just sits there like a doll, looking at the carpet, not saying a word.'

They got married two months later in what must have been the cheapest wedding of the year—Vasant did not approve of expensive weddings. The guests were served exactly one meal. On the plus side—for the guests—they were told to bring no gifts, not even flowers, and certainly not 'envelopes'. Those too were against Vasant's principles. That was not all. For their honeymoon, the two of them did not go to Khandala or wherever (for which the girl's side would have had to shell out the rupees). Vasant had the master bedroom in his flat decked up with strings of flowers for the occasion.

That night, however, when Asha was seated on the marital bed (like Waheeda Rehman in *Chaudhvin ka Chand*, I guess) and (I'm still guessing) Vasant was lifting her chin up, disaster struck. She opened her eyes, saw him...and screamed, yes, screamed. Once, twice, thrice. His mother rushed to the door and started banging on it.

'What happened? What happened?' Her brother (the one who had come from Rajkot for the wedding and not yet gone back) scrambled out of his bed and joined the mother. Full five minutes later, an ashen-faced Vasant opened the door and, for the first time in his life, told a lie.

'Asha saw a cockroach.'

'Oh!' the mother exclaimed, taking a quick step back and looking down. Then, finding no cockroach at her feet, she peered gingerly into the bedroom. Her brother joined her. They saw the bride shrinking into a corner of the bed, still trembling in fright.

'Then that is all right,' her brother said uncertainly. 'Let us go, behn,' he escorted the mother out and closed the door behind them.

There were no more screams that night but Vasant spent it on the floor, by himself. Asha spent it curled up in a corner of the bed in terror, watching out for him to make any sudden move in her direction.

Such things can't be kept hidden from saga-vhalas for long, not in our community. Two more nights and everybody in both the families knew that the marriage had not been consummated, and was not likely to be consummated any time soon. All that Vasant's mother could get out of him was that his bride did not want him anywhere close to her, he did not know why. My sister too would not tell anybody why. Finally it was massi, our mother's elder sister, who ferreted the secret out of her.

'He looks like Pran,' she told massi, 'exactly like him, carbon copy.'

'Pran? Who Pran?'

'Praaan. Don't you know? The villain in *Bari Behen*, *Ram aur Shyam*, and oh, so many films.'

Such news too can't be kept hidden from saga-vhalas.

'Well, he does look like Pran,' said Lata. Lata was our chhota faiba, father's youngest sister. She too saw films.

'For heaven's sake,' father snapped. 'Those are only films!'

'In any case,' faiba said to Asha, 'Pran played only good roles in later life, like a gentleman.'

'But *he* looks like Pran when he was young,' wailed Asha.

'I too would be scared if my husband looked like Pran,' said Shanta, a cousin. 'Once I saw someone looking just like Pran at Kwality's. I couldn't sleep that night.'

It was our grandmother who finally saved the day. 'Just close your eyes, beti,' she counselled Asha, 'and pretend that he is Amitabh Bachchan. How do you think I coped with your grandfather?'

And that is probably what Asha did, closed her eyes. Years passed. They had a son, then a daughter. Vasant became senior accountant, then Assistant Chief Accountant in his company, L&T. Yes, he kept looking troublingly like Pran, the young Pran. For the rest, however, Asha's life was one long domestic bliss. She put on weight. She bought a flat-screen TV. She won a few more quiz contests, including the famous Bournvita contest on film songs. I still recall the answer she gave to the last question, the one about which star 'sang' the song 'Thandi Hawayein', to which composer's tune, in which film, in which year. She not only gave the correct answer (Nalini Jaywant, to music composed by S.D. Burman, in the film *Naujawan*, released in 1951) but also added that though the background singer was Lataji, the one first chosen to sing it was Pushpaji.

'Pushpaji who?' one of the judges, looking thoroughly bewildered, had cried.

'Why,' she had raised an eyebrow, 'Pushpa Hans, of course.'

If anything caused a ripple (I should say, ripples) in their life, it was guests from up-country visiting Bombay and staying with them from time to time. Unfortunately, there was no way to avoid them. They were saga-vhalas. Fortunately, they did not stay for long. Ten days at most. And they took the hint when Asha told them that they were expecting other saga-vhalas the next week. (That is another specialty of our community: we take hints.) I hasten to add that I never imposed myself on Vasant and Asha. I had moved to Delhi after college to work for the Government. We kept in touch and met often but whenever I came to

Bombay, I stayed either with my parents, or, when they too had saga-vhalas from up-country visiting them, in a Government guesthouse in Malabar Hill. Vasant and Asha came to meet me there then, generally with the children. The children loved the food at the guesthouse, with potatoes and onions in every dish. Both items were forbidden at home, along with everything else that grows underground.

~

Once, they visited me without the children. 'I want your advice on something,' Asha said, giving me the reason.

'Fire!' I said encouragingly.

'Kirit and Neha are still with us,' she began immediately, before I had time even to order nimbupani for everybody.

Kirit was our massi's sister-in-law's grandson, twenty-one or twenty-two years of age, a great cricket player—he had played for Saurashtra in several Ranji Trophy matches the previous year—but 'with an empty upper storey', as we said when we talked about him behind his back. Neha was his young wife, pretty as a picture but probably with an equally empty upper storey. They had come to Bombay because Kirit had been promised a job in Godrej, or so massi had written. 'They will be with you for four or five days at most,' she had said. 'They will be moving into the Godrej housing colony in Thane after that.'

Soon after they came to Bombay, however, everybody had realized that Kirit had no job waiting for him. Somebody he had met in Rajkot had told him that companies like Godrej would snap up *like this* a great cricket player like him, and would even give him a flat to live in. The idiot had built castles in the air, turned up in Bombay with his wife and set up camp in Asha's place.

'They have been with us almost two months,' Asha cried.

'Two months!' I was surprised. 'Time flies.'

Asha frowned.

I tried to make amends. 'Er... Why not tell them that you are expecting other guests,' I suggested the time-tested remedy.

'Of course I told them that—told *him*, I should say. She is quiet as a mouse. Doesn't speak a word. Just sits and watches films with me—black-and-white films,' she added unnecessarily.

'And what did he say when you told him that?'

'He asked me who we were expecting. It gave me such a shock. I mean, nobody ever asks such questions. I had to think up a name quickly. I said Sharad uncle. He said it was wonderful news—Sharad uncle was great fun. And he said that in such a peculiar way... As if we are not great fun.'

'I see...' I reconsidered the problem. 'Why not write to massi?' I suggested finally.

'And say what to her?' Asha snapped.

I saw her point.

Everybody waited.

Then, I don't know what got into me but I said, 'I have an idea.'

'What?' she asked.

'Let Vasant flirt with the wife, what's her name? Neha.'

'What!' It was Vasant who cried.

'Nothing serious,' I hastened to assure. 'Just leer at her the way villains do in films...'

'What!'

'Grab her hand when nobody is looking...'

'What what what!'

'Sing a song?'

'Song?'

'Something like, "Ek larki ko dekha to aisa laga",' I added. 'If after that they don't leave, my name is not...'

Asha found her voice at last. 'Have you taken leave of your senses?'

'I...am just trying to help,' I said.

'Help like this? Are you my brother or enemy? Come!' she rose to go. Vasant rose with her at exactly the same instant, like husbands do in Gujarati comedies.

'I say, Asha,' I too rose. 'I was only... I'm sorry if...'

But she was already out of the door and several steps down the staircase. Vasant turned to give me a rueful look, as if to convey that I had just done something that was going to cost him a limb, and scampered after her.

~

Peace in the family returned suddenly a week later. 'Kirit and Neha have left Asha's place,' my mother telephoned me from Bombay that day to tell me.

'Excellent!' I said. But I was curious. I telephoned Asha. Vasant picked up the phone. I could not then help saying what I said. 'I'm glad that you followed my suggestion, Vasant, and switched on your charm before the young lady.'

'Please...' Vasant pleaded, and quickly passed the phone to Asha.

'My congratulations,' I said. 'I understand that the young pests have gone.'

That thawed her a bit.

'Yes,' she said. 'To Ahmedabad. It seems that Kirit has found a job there with some British firm.'

'Good news.'

'Yes. But I wish Ahmedabad was in Assam,' she added, 'not just an overnight train journey from Bombay.'

~

Before the year was out, we had more good news. Kirit had been bought by the Sussex Cricket Club for some astronomical amount. He and his pretty wife had migrated to England. The next thing we heard, from some saga-vhalas who had visited London, was that they had bought a house in Wembley.

Years passed. Asha put on more weight. The children grew up and started going to college. Bombay turned into Mumbai...

Then one day we heard of a poll conducted by the BBC to find out, from its viewers, who was the greatest film villain ever? To the astonishment of the organizers, no villain from Hollywood or England featured anywhere near the top of the list, not even fellows who had played Dracula. All of the first five names were from Bollywood, with Pran topping the list. He received 93,000 votes. Amrish Puri came second with 89,000 votes. K.N. Singh came third... Two days later came some breaking news.

The poll results had been set aside. There had been a fraud. As many as seven thousand of the votes for Pran had been cast by a single individual, tracked down to the email address of one nehakirit@gmail.com

The result? My sister is not talking to me any more. As for Vasant, from what I have heard from a saga-vhala, he has returned to sleeping on the floor.

Her F Word

Although Freny and Madhav had joined college—St Xavier's—the same day, and she was pretty and he handsome, they did not meet each other till many months later. Even in those days, almost thirty years back, Xavier's was the most popular college in Bombay. It overflowed with students.

Moreover, they had little in common. She liked books, films, plays, music…things cultural. She had attended every event of the Malhar music festival of the college that year.

He liked sports, above all, cricket. He had played cricket for his school, and was hopeful that he would be taken in the college team soon.

She lived with her grandmother, parents and a sister in a Parsi housing colony in Wadala. Her father was a doctor in JJ Hospital. Her mother was a teacher.

He lived with his parents, a brother and a sister in a penthouse overlooking the Oval. His father was a High Court lawyer. His mother did not need to work.

In short, there was little chance of their meeting. But they did meet one day, on the 29th of February to be precise. She had just sat down with some friends round a table in the college canteen. He was sitting at the next table, cutting a birthday cake to the singing of 'Happy Birthday to You' by his friends. And one of her friends, a girl everybody called TT (for Tomboy Tanuja) suddenly called out, 'Hey guys! Keep some of the cake for us. It is also Freny's birthday today.'

He turned and saw a blushing girl in a long, pink and white dress sitting on TT's right. Her hair, shoulder-length, was held back by a ribbon of the same shades. Her neck, long and smooth, was bare. He waved a hand and said hi. She raised a hand a few inches from her lap and murmured hi.

'So how about the cake?' TT demanded.

'What? Yes, yes of course.' He scrambled to cut a generous portion of the cake, put it on a plate, walked up to the other table and, holding the plate with both hands, offered it to Freny with a bow.

'Thank you,' she murmured. Her voice was low, a bit husky, nice. 'But this is too much cake…'

'No, it is not,' TT cried, grabbing away the plate before he could say anything.

Everybody laughed.

He shrugged and offered the girl his hand. 'I am Madhav Apte, from First Year Arts.'

'I am Freny Cama, from First Year Science,' she said, placing her hand in his.

The hand was as light as a dove chick he had picked up from a nest once, years back, and just as soft. He let it go gently and said, 'Pleased to meet you.'

'Freny is sweet sixteen today,' TT said. 'What about you? The same?'

'Yes, sixteen,' he turned to her and said, 'but not sweet.'

'Oho! Somebody is fishing,' TT cried, causing another round of laughter.

'Don't mind TT,' Freny said to him softly, 'She only teases people she likes.'

He mumbled a thank you and retreated to his table.

By and by a bell rang. The girls were the first to leave, with a loud 'Thanks for the cake' from TT. His eyes followed Freny to the door. She stopped before walking out and looked back. He gave her a smile. She smiled back, sealing the sudden, magical bond between them.

~

He saw her again only the day the college reopened in June. She was trying to get close to the noticeboard that showed the results of the First Year exams. He had just scanned the pages. 'Hi, Freny,' he shouted over a dozen heads when he saw her. 'You have topped the class!' The heads turned to see her. She blushed. 'You have stood first!' he continued, pushing his way through the crowd.

'First class first,' he cried when he reached her. 'Fantastic!'

'Are you sure?' she asked.

'Of course I'm sure,' he said. 'You are Freny Cama, aren't you? Grandchild of the indomitable freedom fighter, Bhikhaiji Cama.'

'Bhikhaiji Cama had no child.'

'Who said child? I said grandchild.'

She laughed.

'So how about a treat?'

They went to the canteen. But the news had spread and they were no longer alone.

~

They met each other several times in the months that followed, mostly in the canteen, and always with others. She did not speak much, he noticed, or maybe TT did not allow anybody else to speak much, but she smiled, and sometimes laughed, when he said anything amusing. (For example, 'India is overpopulated. We should have stricter population control, starting with the guys in this canteen!')

On their seventeenth birthday—they celebrated it on 28th February this time—he insisted on bringing a cake for everybody, and gave her a book, *Life and Times of Tilak*. 'Tilak was the first real freedom fighter,' he told everybody. She gave him an *Anthology of Indian Poems* by modern Indian poets.

~

One morning he saw her sitting by herself in the canteen, an open book on the table before her.

'Hi!' he said.

'Oh hi!' she looked up.

'I hope I am not disturbing you.'

'No,' she shook her head. 'I was just looking up something.' She closed the book. It was a book on biology, he saw. The annual exams of Second Year Science were beginning two days later, he remembered. Those of Second Year Arts had still a week to go.

'What are you studying Science for?' he took a chair and asked. 'Planning to become a doc?'

'Un-hun,' she nodded.

'Impressed!' he said. 'I wish I had the brains to do Science.'

'You got a high first in CBSE,' she said. 'You could have got into Science like a shot.'

'You have been spying on me!' he said.

'Absolutely!' she said.

'That's terrible… But I confess I too have been sniffing around. And you know what I have discovered?'

'What?'

'That in this huge ocean of boys and girls, the whole college, you and I are the only ones to have been born on the 29th of February.'

'No! Really?'

'Absolutely!' he said, mimicking her.

She laughed, then asked, 'But tell me, why didn't you take Science? Why Arts?'

'My father wants me to become a lawyer and join the family firm. He is a lawyer.'

She studied his face for a moment. 'What do *you* want to become?'

'I want…to serve the country.'

He had never said this to anyone before, not even to himself, but now that he had said it, he realized that that was what he wanted to do: serve the country.

She did not laugh. She did not even ask him why he

wanted to serve the country. She only asked, 'In which way?'

'By joining the IAS, the Administrative Service...'

~

The last paper of the annual exams—Hindi—was common to both the classes. He waited for her outside the hall and offered to walk with her to her bus stop. They spoke about the exams, their friends, the new Shyam Benegal film at Metro...

'What are your plans for the vacation?' he asked her at the bus stop.

'We are going to Panchgani for a few weeks. My aunt has a bungalow there. We should be back by the 15th of May. What about you?'

'Nothing special. I'll be playing a bit of cricket,' he added. He had thought of inviting her to watch the Xavier's vs Wilson College match in the first week of May. There was no point in asking her now. She would be away.

~

He telephoned her on the 15th of May.

'Congratulations!' she said before he could say anything.

He had taken 5 wickets for 34 runs in the match against Wilson College and had been declared Man of the Match.

'There was a photograph of yours in the *Deccan Herald*,' she explained.

'I was lucky,' he said.

'Don't say that in front of TT. She will say you are fishing!'

He laughed.

'I thought of you when I saw an old film on VCR in Panchgani.' She continued, 'It is called *Samadhi*, with Ashok Kumar and Nalini Jaywant. It is about Subhas Chandra Bose's Indian National Army marching from Singapore to India to fight the British… You look a little like Ashok Kumar, you know.'

'Not Dev Anand?'

She laughed. 'No, not Dev Anand. Only Ashok Kumar…'

'A pity, that!'

'Not really,' she said and hastened to continue, 'The film has a most moving version of that great song, "Kadam kadam badhaye ja".'

They spoke about other patriotic songs, and agreed that the greatest of them all was 'Sare jahan se achchha'… It brought tears to one's eyes.

'And I'm proud of you,' suddenly she added, 'that you want to serve the country!… You must see *Samadhi* someday.'

When he put down the phone at last, his mother asked him who he was talking to for twenty-two whole minutes. A friend, he said.

'…It sounded like a girl's voice,' she said.

'You are imagining things, aai,' he said.

'What were you talking about?' she asked.

'Cricket,' he said. She gave him a suspicious look. He realized he would have to be careful in future. No telephoning Freny when his mother was around. She had the ears of an elephant. And though she did not know English, she could follow it by instinct.

~

To no one's surprise, Freny stood first in the Second Year Science exams.

They met more frequently in the third year, mostly with the others but increasingly by themselves. He accompanied her to several events of the Malhar festival that year. She went to see him play cricket in the matches against other colleges. After the matches they walked to Chowpatty to celebrate his haul of wickets with panipuri, topping that with a banana split for two at Vibgyor Ice-cream Parlour. Sometimes they went for a Hindi film, or to a Parsi or Irani restaurant she knew, or just travelled up and down the Marine Drive on a bus, sitting on the front seat of the upper deck. And they talked—about the film they had just seen, their college, their professors, their friends, themselves...

He wanted to see India become great again in his lifetime, he said to her. He would be disappointed if he did not succeed in getting into the IAS. It was the toughest exam in India. Lakhs appeared in it every year. Just a hundred or so were selected.

'You could teach...' she suggested.

'Tee-each! My father would have a fit!—and say that he earns more money in ten minutes than a teacher does in six months in school... Maybe I should have taken Science, and become a doctor.'

'That would have been...nice. You would have made a very good surgeon. You have good hands.'

'Oh I don't know. I don't much fancy the idea of chopping up bodies... But tell me, why do *you* want to become a doctor?'

'All my life I have wanted to become a doctor.'

'Nothing else?'

'Nothing else—by way of work, I mean,' she added, looking steadily into his eyes.

'Lucky you… Oh well, I'm too old to switch to Science now. So Law for me if I don't get into the IAS. Or cricket. They too serve who bat and bowl,' he said.

She laughed.

~

On their eighteenth birthday, he gave her Nehru's *Discovery of India*.

She gave him *Anthology of Indian Poems Volume II*.

She stood first in the Third Year exams too.

Time passed quickly in the fourth year, with Malhar, films, walks, talks, restaurants, cricket… During the October holidays that year, they went on a college trip to Mysore. There, while walking behind the others by the floodlit fountains of Vrindavan gardens, she put her arm in his. He was telling her the story of how, miraculously, he had taken six wickets for the Maharashtra cricket team in the Ranji Trophy match against Gujarat. His voice tapered off and by and by he fell silent. They walked thus, in silence, till they came within sight of the waiting bus. She slipped her hand out of his, went into the bus first and sat with the other girls. He sat with the boys.

On their nineteenth birthday, celebrated again on the 28th of February, he brought a cake for everybody, as was almost expected of him now, and gave her a book called *A History of the Marathas*. 'The British did not take India from the Mughals, you know,' he said to everybody. 'They took it from the Marathas. The book tells you all about it.' She gave him Tagore's *Gitanjali*.

'I hope you will skim though this book at least,' she teased. He promised to read it from cover to cover.

'Read it after the Finals,' she said.

He pointed out that the exams were still more than six weeks away. There was enough time to prepare for them.

'Freny is already prepared for them,' TT interjected, 'but she is taking no chances…for you!'

Everybody laughed.

~

'We are only friends,' Freny said to TT later, when they were alone.

'What! Still just friends? You have a lot of catching up to do,' TT laughed, 'after the Finals, of course.'

~

Then disaster struck. Two days before the Finals, Freny came down with pneumonia. The day the exams began she was in a daze of high fever, faintness and antibiotics. The daze stayed with her the whole week of the exams.

'How do you think you have fared?' he asked her after the last paper.

'Okay, I hope,' she said. She did not tell him that she had passed out during the crucial Biology Part II paper and so had not completed it.

'Good. I'll call you when I come back,' he said.

He was going to Chandigarh for a Ranji Trophy match, she knew, and after the match, to the Himalayas for two weeks of trekking with some friends.

'Take care,' she said.

The results of the Finals came out before he had returned. The next thing everybody knew, Freny had dropped out of sight. He tried to get her on the telephone. Her sister said she had gone out of town.

His mother asked him who this Freny was. Freny was short for Framroze, he said, a friend he played cricket with. She gave him a suspicious look. He shrugged and called TT to ask her if she had any news of Freny. She said that Freny had been unable to get into any medical college in Bombay, and had gone to Madras to try to get admission in a college there. It was doubtful if she would succeed. The cutoff marks for all medical colleges in the country were unusually high that year. She herself had just managed to get into the KMC…

His mother asked him who this TT was. 'Tantia Tope,' he snapped. His mother did not speak with him for the rest of the day.

A few days later he tried to get Freny again on the telephone and finally wrote her a letter, conveying that he had joined Government Law College, and asking her what she was doing these days. She sent him a brief reply wishing him all the best in Law, but saying nothing about herself. He telephoned her again. She was not at home.

Some weeks passed. Then months. He visited St Xavier's from time to time to see the few old friends who were still studying there, doing MA, but he also always went to the canteen, and sat there by himself for a while, hoping she would turn up. She never did. He gave up going to Xavier's…

...till the morning of the 29th of February, when all of a sudden he felt he must rush to the old college. He took a taxi. She was waiting for him in the canteen, looking as pretty as ever, though terribly pale.

'What have you been doing with yourself all these months?' he cried. 'I...all of us have been missing you so much.'

'I've been travelling,' she said, 'trying to get admission into a medical college somewhere—anywhere—in India.'

He waited.

'No luck,' she sighed. 'They are all too busy to look at my overall performance and not just the results in the Finals. So last month I also applied to a few medical colleges abroad.'

'Oh!'

'I've just received a telegram from King's College in London, accepting me.'

He fell silent.

'They've offered me a scholarship.'

'Congratulations,' he murmured.

'I have to join them next week.'

'Oh!'

'It's a five-and-a-half-year course,' she said, 'but I can return after four and a half and do my internship in Bombay.'

'More likely, you will meet some nice Englishman...' he said, a sudden bitterness in his voice.

'What!'

'...get married...'

'What!'

'...settle down in dear old England,' he continued, 'give up your Indian citizenship...'

'No!' she cried. 'I will always remain an Indian...'

'...forget us...'

'I'll never forget...anybody.'

~

Her letter to him from London two weeks later conveyed that London was a cold, eternally grey and eternally wet place, and that she missed India more than she had thought she ever would.

His reply to her said that everybody in Bombay missed her. He did not add that he had stopped going to St Xavier's, Metro, the Marine Drive, Chowpatty, Parsi restaurants, and every other place that reminded him of her. He also did not tell her that he hated Medicine—for taking her so far away.

~

She wrote to him every week, conveying how much she missed everyone, and asking him a hundred questions about Bombay, India, himself... He wrote to her less frequently.

A year passed. Then one more year. He hardly ever wrote to her now. There was nothing worthwhile to write about anyway. He had failed in the IAS exams. He had been dropped from the Maharashtra cricket team for not taking a wicket in three matches. He hated Government Law College. He hated Law. Should he join the army? Some NGO? Some newspaper?... Then a friend told him that the only way to pass the IAS exams was to join a good coaching class. They knew what questions to expect and how to prepare for them. He joined a coaching class, learnt by rote readymade answers to questions expected to be asked that year, and appeared in the IAS exams a second time.

He failed again, falling short by three marks. 'Three measly marks,' he wrote in a letter to Freny, his first in months, 'out of a total of 1,500 marks. By way of consolation, they have offered to take me in the Indian Police Service. My father wants me to accept the offer, and opt for the Maharashtra cadre. He says that the family could do with a police officer of its own in Bombay. I don't know if I should. I hate the thought of being useful to the family. Half of India's problems are caused by people who want to be useful to their families.'

'I have accepted the offer,' his second letter to her the same week said. 'I'm joining the Police Service, but I've opted for the Delhi (Union Territory) cadre—and thereby away from the clutches of the family!'

Her long reply consisted of a flurry of questions. He attempted to answer them but gave up after some time. Suddenly he had no time to write letters. He had to fill in forms, book tickets, get clothes stitched, attend farewell parties, give a newspaper interview to a Marathi daily, go to Mussoorie for training, then Hyderabad for more training: study manuals, ride horses, fire weapons, pass exams…

He was quickly identified in the training academy as a high flyer. He rode so well that they took him in the Hyderabad Police Polo team. He shot so well—he could hit a moving six by six inches target with a pistol from a distance of twenty feet—that he represented the police in the national shooting championship that year, getting a gold and a bronze. And he stood first in the written exams at the end of the training.

But he soon learnt when, the training over, he was sent to Delhi on his first assignment, that what he had been taught had little to do with real life. Real life was a snake pit. And the most venomous snakes in it were the all-powerful IAS fellows. They did no real work, save only that which added to their power and perks, and they did not let others work. Bastards. To beat them, one had to have influence; one had to know snakes bigger than them, and the only snakes bigger than them were the politicians. Was there any among them that he could get close to? He checked up the backgrounds of all the politicians from Maharashtra in Delhi; none of them seemed promising.

Then he got his first break. At the wedding of a batch-mate from Madhya Pradesh he heard a girl speaking in Marathi. Someone told him that her name was Urmila and that she was the daughter of the Deputy Chief Minister of MP. Many Marathas had come to the territory as conquerors in the eighteenth century and stayed put. She was unmarried.

He decided to marry her. His parents hesitated—the girl was a Kshatriya, not a Brahmin—but they came round. Her family's position and wealth made up for the lack of caste. Her father too hesitated—the boy was in the IPS and not the more prestigious IAS—but he too came round. The boy had fire in his belly. He was bound to go far. In any case he was a Brahmin, so the girl would be going up in status anyway.

He wrote to Freny about his marriage plans and invited her to the wedding. His letter crossed hers, sent from Bombay, saying that she had come to India for her grandmother's funeral and it would be nice if they could meet. If he wished, she could redirect her return ticket to London via Delhi, spend a couple of days with him there. She had a surprise for him, the letter added, a CD of *Samadhi*, probably pirated!

Her next letter, sent from London some weeks later, conveyed her congratulations—and regrets that she would not be able to attend his wedding. Her MBBS Finals were being held around the same time... She sent him a card, a gift and a bouquet of Interflora flowers on the wedding day. It was the grandest wedding Bhopal had seen in years, full of cards, gifts and bouquets of flowers.

~

His second break came within days of his return to Delhi from a honeymoon in Goa. He was on duty at the High Court in Patiala House. A baba, religious leader, was being tried by the court for a cartload of crimes ranging from tax evasion to rape to murder. There was nothing special about the trial. People were tried for crimes like those every day. Suddenly, however, a huge crowd of the baba's supporters, numbering several hundreds, many of them armed with sticks and swords, descended on the court, determined to wreck the place and free their baba. They smashed windows of a passing bus, set on fire a few stalls outside the gate, chased away all hawkers and passers-by, and attacked the constables on duty, killing one of them on the spot, injuring several and sending the rest fleeing. The inspector-in-charge phoned the SP for help.

And Madhav stepped out—alone. The crowd paused when they saw him, not because he was in uniform: belt, pistol, boots and all. It was the way he stood, and the way he stared at them. Then somebody shouted '*Maro saale ko* (Kill him)' and the crowd surged forward. He pulled out his pistol and waited till they were twenty feet from him; then he fired, not in the air as his training manual had taught him, but into the crowd, selecting his targets. By the time the smoke cleared, there was no one from the crowd left at the scene, save six of their ringleaders, and they were dead, shot through the heart.

Within minutes he was besieged by reporters, press photographers, TV camera crew...asking him to tell the nation what had happened. He did not tell them that he had contempt for all godmen, all lawyers and judges, all self-seeking, greedy politicians and their IAS accomplices...all the people that held India back, and that he was thinking of all of them when he fired into the crowd. He only said that he was doing his duty, that of upholding the law; anybody else in his place would have done the same.

'Weren't you afraid—even for a moment?' a breathless young woman from a TV channel asked him in the end.

'You don't feel afraid,' he replied, 'when you are doing the right thing.'

The story made breaking news on all TV channels, and headlines in all newspapers the next morning. A number of telephone calls between Delhi and Bhopal followed. For twenty-four hours it was a toss-up between suspending him for using disproportionate force and commending him for bravery. In the end the Government decided to commend him. A week later he was transferred to the Prime Minister's office as Security Officer. He would be one of the half a dozen Security Officers there, and he would be the youngest. However, he would report directly to the Deputy Chief Security Officer in any matter involving the security of the PM. It was the most important job in the world, they told him, and the most difficult. They were right. His day began at eight in the morning and ended at ten, six days a week, sometimes seven. He had no time for his personal life any more.

He found time, however, to read a letter from Freny a year later, conveying that she had passed her MBBS exams and was getting married—to Brian Grey, who too was a doctor, some years senior to her, and at the same hospital, King's. He sent her back a reply conveying his congratulations—and reminding her that he had predicted that she would marry an Englishman. A PS at the end of the letter asked her to let him know when she was going to give up her Indian nationality and become British!

Time passed.

Freny got an MS in Paediatrics. Brian became a consultant. They had a son, then a daughter, then one more son.

Madhav too had a son. He was a good boy, affectionate. From time to time Madhav felt guilty that he had such little time for him. Urmila too led a busy life, full of friends, relatives, shops, clubs... Luckily, they had good servants; and, of course, the boy went to the best schools in Delhi:

Magic Years when he turned three, Modern Elementary when he turned five, Sanskriti when he turned ten…

That year was a lucky year for Madhav too. He became Deputy Chief Security Officer when the incumbent was transferred to the Indian embassy in Washington. He knew that in making him the DCSO, the Government had bypassed dozens of officers senior to him, all of whom must hate him now. But what the hell, he was better at the job than all of them put together.

The only problem was that the Prime Minister he was serving was not good at *his* job. Actually, all the Prime Ministers he had served in his twelve years in the PMO had disappointed him. He had not minded them being more or less corrupt. That was the price the country had to pay for being a democracy. What troubled him was that they were all weak and indecisive, scared of their own shadows, and therefore doing none of the things that needed to be done to make India great again. He was serving pygmies.

A few more years passed. Then one day the Chief Security Officer was killed in a failed bomb attack on the Prime Minister. The Prime Minister was new to the job, but he had come to it with a reputation of being a tough, no-nonsense man, just the man the country needed, especially now, when it was plagued with problems, internal as well as external. He was also totally incorruptible. His supporters adored him. His enemies wanted him dead. The bomb attack on him was at least the third attempt on him in the last ten years of his public life.

They made Madhav, the 'fearless Maratha' as the press called him, the Chief Security Officer. Now he was both hated as well as feared. He enjoyed that. A mere telephone call from him sent senior IAS officers scurrying to do his bidding. Even cabinet ministers.

What he did not enjoy was the PM doing anything out of the ordinary, for that meant taking risks. He would have liked the PM to confine himself to going from his Race Course Road residence to his South Block office in the morning and returning to the residence in the evening—with an occasional trip to the Parliament House. But the man preferred to mix with the crowds, especially during election time. And it was always election time somewhere or the other in the country. Life became a nightmare then. The only way to ensure his security was to prepare for every possible eventuality.

Madhav prepared for that. He got the right men to head RAW, IB, Delhi Police...other bodies. He got them to make lists of all groups, internal as well as external, which might wish to kill the PM. He created an army of informers to track the activities of the groups in the lists. He got another army of computer whiz-kids to hack into their emails. He got every suspicious phone tapped and every letter opened. He tightened every rule that governed the issuance of passports and visas by Indian missions abroad. He trusted no one, not even the people who worked for him, nor the ones who had sworn eternal allegiance to the PM. He never forgot that a former PM had been killed by her own bodyguards.

~

One day, the PM decided to visit London. Actually, the British had sent the invitation to the previous PM. But that made no difference. In fact, the British were happy that it would be the new PM visiting London. He was more powerful, and therefore more important to cultivate. There were a number of trade and investment agreements to be finalized and signed between the two governments. The British prepared a three-day programme for him, crowded with public engagements: a ceremonial reception; a high tea at Buckingham Palace; a luncheon by the British PM; a cocktail party in the Indian High Commissioner's residence; a formal banquet; a gala reception by the large Asian (i.e. Indian community) in London; a press conference, two TV interviews; a ceremonial departure...

Madhav liked the programme; it was time that India was treated with the respect it deserved, especially in Britain. Maybe someday India would also be able to extract from the British an apology for the devastation their long rule had caused in India. But the programme was also a security nightmare. The British High Commissioner in Delhi asked him to leave everything to British security. They knew their job, he said. No way, Madhav said. India must be consulted and have the final say in the security arrangements. He even reminded the High Commissioner of the incident some years back, when the IRA had come within a hair's breadth of killing almost the entire British cabinet. As you wish, said the High Commissioner in the end. Madhav said thank you, and added that he wished to make a visit to London to go over the proposed security arrangements. These had to be foolproof.

They invited him to London for a working visit and sent him a detailed programme for it. The programme was all right, he felt. He would be meeting the right people, and going to the right places but his evening—his only evening in London—was kept free... It would be silly to spend it in his hotel room. Was there anybody in London he knew? Of course he did. Freny! He had not written to her in years. Her Christmas cards too had stopped coming... He got her number from TT in Bombay (now rightly renamed Mumbai) and telephoned her. She invited him to dinner and offered to ask her husband to pick him up from his hotel. He said not to worry; he would have a car. 'We live in St John's Wood,' she said, 'not very far from the Strand,' and gave him the address.

The first thing that he discovered when he sat down for talks with his British counterparts was that the security arrangements that they had made were far from foolproof. The worst were the arrangements at the most vulnerable place, the hotel where the PM was going to stay. They had made no plans to sanitize the surroundings. Nor had they looked into the fact that the hotel had a large number of 'Asian' employees, brown people. That was unpardonable.

Madhav told them that no 'Asian' should be allowed to enter the hotel, let alone work there during the three days the PM would be there. As the whole world knew, London was a hotbed of anti-India terrorists of every type—Pakistanis, Bangladeshis, Nepalese, Kashmiris, Muslims, Sikhs, Tamils, Sinhalese, leftists, rightists... You name it, London had it. And there was no way to know who was a terrorist and who was not. So the best course was to keep all Asian men away from the hotel. Women too; an Indian Prime Minister had been killed by a woman suicide bomber. Yellow men too; any of them could be a Naga or a Mizo or an Assamese. Blacks too; they were inherently violent. In short, he said, only white waiters should be allowed to work in the hostel those three days. And only white people should be allowed to enter it, except those cleared by him personally.

'How can we do that?' they pleaded. 'There would be an uproar in the country if we did that.'

Too bad, he said. But if they did not put those restrictions in place, the visit would be off. It was blunt talk, he knew, but it was the only kind of talk that the British understood. In any case, the British were in no position to say no to anything he asked for. The deals that the PM was going to finalize during his London visit would earn the British three and a half billion pounds, perhaps more. They would sell their grandmothers for that much money. As Napoleon had famously said, they were just a nation of shopkeepers. Not like the Marathas.

Then there was the question of tightening up the security cordon round the High Commission of India, which the PM would be visiting, and round the Indian High Commissioner's residence, and the… It was almost seven-thirty when he decided to call it a day and resume his talks the next morning. They still had to go over the security arrangements for the parade and, worst of all, the gala reception by the Indian community. He wished he could strike out the reception. Alas, the PM himself wanted to address the thirty thousand overseas Indians expected to assemble there.

He reached St John's Wood at almost nine. He had

no difficulty in finding the place. Freny's directions were precise. And a well-lit board at the gate of the house read: 'Freny and Brian live here'.

She looked young for—how old?—his own age, of course, a forty-five-year-old, though a bit fuller than he had remembered her. Brian, her husband, was slimmer, taller, balding and with slightly drooping shoulders. How old would he be? Fifty-five? More? It was difficult to tell. Europeans often looked older than they were. But he was affable, and generous with his rare double malt whisky, sorely needed after the hard day's work. And soon they were chatting away, about Britain, India, Indo-British relations, the latest crisis in the Middle East... The children joined them for a few minutes, but only to be introduced. They had had their dinner and soon took their leave.

The dinner consisted entirely of Indian dishes—even the soup: a bowl of rasam! He asked Freny if she always ate Indian food.

Brian replied for her. 'There are five things of India that Freny has always missed. All of them begin with the letter F. Food is one of them.'

'What are the other Fs?'

'Family.'

'Yes?'

'Friends.'

'Yes?'

'Films.'

'Yes?'

Brian paused.

'So what is the fifth F?' Madhav asked.

'Not what you might think it is...' Brian said, his eyes twinkling in mischief. 'She gets enough of *that* with me.'

Freny blushed to the root of her hairs.

'Sorry, Freny!' Brian laughed. 'Oh, shall we tell him about our visit to the Indian High Commission last May?'

'There is nothing to tell,' she said.

'What visit?' Madhav asked. 'What happened at the High Commission, Freny?'

She commenced reluctantly. 'I had just received a message saying that my father had suffered a heart attack and had been hospitalized. I threw some clothes in a suitcase and Brian called our travel agent to book a seat for me on the first available flight to Mumbai. We were on the road in fifteen minutes. It was when we were almost at Heathrow—Brian was driving the car—that he asked me to check if my passport was in order,' she paused. 'It was not!'

Brian continued, as if on cue. 'It was an Indian passport. I had often asked her to change it, get a British passport, I mean. It is murder to try and go anywhere on short notice with an Indian passport. For it requires visas to go to even France, and those can take ages. She had refused to change it...'

'You don't need visas for India if you have an Indian passport,' Madhav said dryly.

'Quite right,' Brian agreed. 'Her problem this time was different. Her passport had expired. So I took a U-turn and headed for the Indian High Commission. I knew the way,' he laughed. 'We have visited the place twice a year every year—on Republic Day and Independence Day, to watch the hoisting of the flag, listen to the speech of the Indian

High Commissioner—and top off the outing with pakoras and chai.

'There was "No parking" near the High Commission, so I sat in the car near the entrance—telling a bobby on duty there that it would be only for ten or fifteen minutes. And Freny got out of the car and ran in… She came back in fifteen minutes all right, but in tears, and without the passport extended.'

'Why?' Madhav asked Freny.

'The man at the counter refused to extend it,' she murmured. 'He said that under the rules, he had to get the approval of the issuing office—in my case, the Mumbai RPO—before extending the validity. That could take months. I told him that I could not wait; my father was in ICU. "So what can *I* do about it?" the man said. "You overseas Indians are all like this only. You come to us at the last minute—after the last minute—and want us to give you the moon."'

'He asked you for a bribe, right? Did you get his name? I—'

'The story is not over yet,' Brian said.

'I… Hmm.'

Brian continued the story, 'It was while we were talking—I mean I was asking questions and Freny was sobbing—that the bobby, who was still standing near the car, coughed and said, "I could not help overhearing you, sir, madam… May I offer a suggestion?"'

'"What?" both of us cried.

'"Let the gentleman go in with the passport," the bobby said, "and ask for it to be extended."

'Freny and I stared at him uncomprehendingly for a moment. Then I got out of the car, collected the passport and the form from Freny and went in.'

'So what happened?' Madhav asked.

'You tell him, Freny!'

Freny sighed and took over, 'Brian came out ten minutes later—with the passport duly extended.'

'So Brian paid the man the bribe…' Madhav said.

'No,' Brian replied. 'I did not have to pay anybody any bribe. My white face was enough!'

It was some moments later that Madhav spoke again. 'I expect Freny has acquired a British passport now.'

'Alas, she has not. She still has her Indian passport. That reminds me, Freny, we will have to get you visas for the conference in Sweden next week.'

~

He gave Freny a peck on her cheek before saying goodbye at the door. Brian walked with him to the car.

'I must thank you,' he said to Madhav as they walked.

'For what?'

'For not marrying Freny. That gave me the chance to become the happiest man in England.'

'But there was never anything between Freny and me.'

'Oh come now. She was in love with you for years. Probably still is. She even proposed to you in writing.'

'What! When?'

'On your nineteenth birthday, inside the book she gave you.'

He remembered the book: Tagore's *Gitanjali*. He had never even opened it.

'How do you know this?'

'I read her diary. I know I should not have. But I did. It made me terribly jealous of you, but also terribly happy when I realized what a gem she is: "lakhon me ek", as some Bollywood film song goes.'

They reached the car.

'So what is the fifth F she misses of India?' Madhav asked him as the driver opened the door.

'Didn't I tell you? The fifth F is the flag of India,' Brian said. 'Tears spring to her eyes every time she watches it being unfurled.'

~

He was not sure if he had kept the book. He looked for it when he reached Delhi. It was still there, though with the jacket gone, and with stains on the edges of the pages. He opened it. And there they were, her words on the yellowed fly page.

An offering from
(hopefully some day)
yours forever
F

Like Gandhi

It must be my name, Mohandas Gandhi. I can think of no other reason why, every time I fly out of Mumbai, no matter by what airline, they serve me Indian vegetarian food—soggy cauliflower, undercooked daal, sad-looking rice, rubbery chapatis, dried-up salad, nondescript pickles... They also serve me before everybody else. The plane has barely reached cruising altitude when some air hostess or the other rushes up to me, the tray in hand, and with the air of one who is doing me a special favour, offers it to me. I tell her that I don't want the favour. I want normal food, that's to say, what the others are going to get: chicken, fish, meat...preferably cooked in some sensible, logical way (French if I am travelling by Air France, German if I am travelling by Lufthansa...).

And I like a drink—two drinks—before food, I tell her. She says she is not in charge of drinks. She is only in charge of meals and she is giving me the special meal I had asked for, she adds, plonking the tray before me. I lift the silver foil hiding the dish to see if it is what I suspect it is. It is. It always is. I stab it with the forefinger of my right hand and say that I would have to be an idiot to ask for *that*. She purses her lips and whips out a list of passengers. See, she says, pointing to the letters HVF written in ink against my name. Hindu Vegetarian Food, she explains. You have got the wrong man, I say, I am not a vegetarian. I have never been a vegetarian since the day I was born, seventy years back, I add. She looks at the list again and asks, aren't you Mo-Hun-Dash-Gan-Di? I say yes, but... Then this is your food, she says triumphantly, rolling up the list. No! I cry, raising my voice. That is not my food. Yes, I am a Hindu. Yes, my name is Gandhi. But I am not a vegetarian. And that is not my food. I never ordered it.

That brings reinforcements—on her side. The new air hostess, clearly the senior of the two (though the first one is no chicken), asks what is the matter. I tell her what is the matter. The other shows the senior the list. Hmm, says the senior. Then she looks at the number of the seat I am sitting on and matches it with the number in the list. Then she purses her lips and asks me if my name is not Gandhi (she pronounces it Ghan-di). I say yes, but... She declares that in that case the food is mine and I should eat it. I say I will not. I insist on being given what the others are going to be served, chicken, fish, meat...anything normal. Hmm, she says, pursing her lips again. Then she says she will see if any food is left after the others have been served. And she departs. The first one then takes away the tray. I wait.

By and by the drinks trolley comes. I grab a beer before they can ask me whether I want a Coke or Pepsi, these being things that (in the eyes of the world) go with Hindu Vegetarian Food. They watch my every move while serving the normal food to the others, as if they are afraid that I might grab one of the packets. I only ask for one more beer, get it, and wait. Some days a chicken dish is left and I get that; mostly nothing is left and they offer to bring back the Hindu food tray. Go to hell, I say, clenching my teeth.

Within hours of being back on terra firma, I send a long complaint to the general manager of the airline. I don't forget to add that I am chairman of Gandhi Solar Energy, Mumbai, the best-known offshoot of Gandhi Hardware, also founded by me. He writes back some days later saying that he does not know how the mix-up could have occurred. He promises me that it will not occur again. He assures me that I am an esteemed and valuable customer of the airline.

I shrug—time has calmed me down by then—and forget the whole thing. Till the next time. The mix-up occurs again, and again, even though I keep complaining, keep getting reassurances from the chairmen and keep changing airlines. A friend tells me the problem is deeper. There has been a surge in recent years in the interest of the world in Mahatma Gandhi and his philosophy. Indeed there is not a country in the world—and therefore not an airline in the world—that does not know that Gandhi was a confirmed vegetarian. Moreover, at seventy years of age I *have* begun to look a bit like him. Maybe I should change my name, he suggests.

I consider the suggestion. I do need to travel often. It is frustrating not to get proper food while travelling. My chartered accountant—I have known him since school—advises me not to give the suggestion a thought. The shares of all the Gandhi group of companies could take a dive if I did that. Names matter, he adds. Would Gandhiji still be called the Father of the Nation if he had changed his name to, say, Lalu Yadav? Why not travel by First Class instead? he suggests. Or Club Class? As the 107th richest man in Mumbai, he adds with a smile, I can afford it.

I say that I would rather give the money to charity. It is a waste of money to travel by First or Club Class. Surely, I can easily handle the small discomforts of Economy class for a few hours. And I am fit. I walk two miles every day, play tennis every weekend, eat decent, muscle-building food: chicken, fish, meat...! Then I give him the clinching argument. You say I am the 107th richest man in Mumbai. I say, so how do you expect me to become even the 106th richest man in Mumbai if I waste my money?

In that case, he suggests, maybe you should cut down on non-vegetarian food. You are not young any more, you know, he adds.

You are my friend, I say, giving him a stern look. Don't try and become my wife. He laughs. He is a married man. Mercifully, I am not.

And for your information, I tell him, seventy is today's fifty.

But the problem of food while flying remains. I tell every airline, weeks before the day of the flight, that I am not a vegetarian, and that I like sensible, local food. I send them daily reminders till the day of the flight. Sometimes, the strategy works, mostly it doesn't.

~

Last week I had to go to Los Angeles on sudden work. The cheapest fare was that of South China Airlines. But the flight would leave at an unearthly hour—3 am—my secretary warned me. And I would have to change flights at Guangzhou after a four-hour stopover. No problem, I said. Just make sure that I get proper food on the plane on both sectors, normal food, no daal-chawal. And beer. Chinese beer.

They did have Chinese beer on the flight, actually Hong Kong beer, Tsingtao, one of the best beers in Asia. I gulped down the first can, as is my style, and sipped the second one slowly, savouring every mouthful. Then, my quota of beer over, I asked the air hostess for the food. Local food! I reminded her.

'Yes sir,' she nodded breathlessly, as only the young on their first jobs can. I looked at her. How old would she be? Seventeen? Eighteen? She was pretty, like all hostesses should be, and slim, like all Chinese girls are. God knows where they find them. (I am not a sex maniac. There was a time when… But that was a long time back. My interest in sex now is purely visual, and in little girls, entirely grandfatherly.)

She returned with a tray—of rice, soggy cauliflower, daal, chapatis, dried-up salad and pickles!

And something snapped in me. I exploded. 'What rubbish is this?' I shouted. 'I had asked for real food, local food, Chinese food.'

'But we have no Chinese food,' she took a step back.

'What!' I shouted. 'No Chinese food on China Airlines?'

A steward appeared. 'That's right, sir,' he said. 'We do not serve Chinese food on the Mumbai-Guangzhou sector, only Hindu food. Our passengers want that only. We get it fresh in Mumbai,' he added.

'Well, you could have got some fresh Chinese food too,' I snapped. 'There are plenty of restaurants in Mumbai that serve excellent Chinese food.'

The steward looked away, embarrassed.

The penny dropped. 'At least *good* Chinese food,' I muttered, modifying the praise. 'It is cheating,' I continued, 'not to serve Chinese food in a China Airlines flight.'

'We will make note of that for future, sir,' he bowed stiffly and left, leaving the field to the air hostess.

'I had told your management that I wanted Chinese food,' I said, still simmering. 'Take away this…this…and get me some Chinese food.'

'But we have no Chinese food on this flight,' she wailed.

'Then I will not eat,' I folded my arms and stared at something far away. Mahatma Gandhi could not have done better before announcing his fast unto death.

Consternation. She looked left and right, and at me again. I stayed firm.

'Will you have dim sum and noodles, sir?' she asked uncertainly. 'It is simple food, not very…'

'Yes, I will have it,' I unfolded the arms.

Soon the plate arrived. It wasn't much food, just three small dim sum offerings and a bowl of boiled noodles, but it was all right. I said so to her, and added, unable to resist the impulse to bite, 'You told me there was no Chinese food on the plane. How did you find this?'

'It is my food, sir,' she murmured, looking down. 'I am so glad that you liked it.'

'Oh!' I said. 'What will you eat?'

'I am not hungry, sir,' she said.

~

She was at the exit of the plane to say goodbye to the passengers in the morning. I saw from the label on her shoulder that her name was Xiang Syau Xing?

'What does it mean?' I asked her, pointing at the name.

'Xiang is the family name, sir,' she bowed.

'And the other two names?'

'They mean Making Happy, sir,' she said.

By a Thread

'There was a call for you from Mrs Meherali, sir,' his PA told him when he returned from lunch.

'Meherali?' Rahul tried to recall if he had met anybody by that name. As First Secretary (Culture) in the High Commission of India in Islamabad, he met a lot of people.

'She said she was calling from Rawalpindi, sir,' the PA added.

In that case, it was unlikely that he had met her, he decided. He would have remembered the name. He met very few people from Rawalpindi. Nor did he often go there himself, although it was less than an hour away. The place made him uncomfortable: it was the headquarters of the Pakistani army; and there was no love lost between the Pakistani army and the High Commission of India—especially First Secretary (Culture), whose job it was to strengthen cultural ties between India and Pakistan. The Pakistani army, if it could have its way, would undo even the few cultural ties that existed between the two countries. It was still smarting from its defeat in the last war against India and wanted revenge, not better relations.

No, the caller was probably only someone who wanted visas for India. Nine times out of ten the calls that he got—

that all officers in the High Commission got—were from people wanting visas. Time was when the bulk of the visas were issued by the Indian Consulate in Karachi, which made sense. Under the Indo-Pak visa agreement, mostly only Pakistanis with relatives in India were entitled to visit India. And so, almost by definition, they were muhajirs, people who had migrated from India to Pakistan after the Partition and settled down in Karachi and other towns in Sind. It suited them to get the visas in Karachi. But during one of the periodic dips in Indo-Pak relations, the Indian Consulate in Karachi had been forced to close down. And although relations between the two countries had improved somewhat since then, Pakistan had not allowed India to reopen the Consulate. All the visa work was now being handled by the High Commission in Islamabad…

…with the result that the visa section of the High Commission had become the busiest visa office anywhere in the world. People gathered in front of its gates before six in the morning. At nine, when the gates opened, they poured in like water from a burst dam. Over a thousand people applied for visas every day. It was a tough job even to maintain order before the visa windows. Just the other day the stampede of visa seekers had almost killed an old woman. She was saved only because a burly security guard had noticed what was happening and rushed to her aid.

The High Commission had neither the space nor the staff to handle the huge workload. All applications went to Delhi for processing and approval. The clerks at the windows only collected the applications, scanned them to make sure that they were filled correctly and sent away the applicants, advising them to wait for the reply from Delhi—which could take months. Not believing this to be true, many applicants stayed on in Islamabad, camping on a huge, dusty plot of land across the road from the High Commission, washing there, cooking there, defecating in the open there…even, in a couple of instances, dying there—and adding to the chaos before the visa windows when those opened for business. Inevitably, the smarter applicants tried to avoid the whole dismaying experience by approaching officers directly.

'Did she say what she wanted?' he asked his PA.

'Yes, sir. She wanted to know if you were a Gujarati.'

'What!… What on earth for?'

'I asked her that, sir. She said she will tell you why. From me she only wanted to know if you were a Gujarati, since many non-Gujaratis also have the surname Bhat.'

'And what did you tell her?'

'I told her that I did not know if you were a Gujarati, and would have to check that up. She will call back after lunch, sir.'

A perfect PA, Arora, always alert, always protecting him from callers, never conveying more information than was absolutely necessary…

'She is probably interested in visas,' Rahul shrugged and said.

'Er… I don't think so, sir.'

'N-o…? Why?'

'Because she said that I should not trouble you if you were not a Gujarati.'

'Do you mean to say that she does not want to talk with me if I am not a Gujarati?'

'Yes, sir.'

Rahul wondered what to make of the call. It could be a ploy to get visas. Or…wait a minute, it could be a honey trap. Pakistan's ISI was notorious for trying to snare Indian officials through its female operatives. And by now probably everybody in ISI knew that his wife had stayed on in Delhi with the children, so for all practical purposes he was single in Islamabad.

The phone rang. He picked it up before his PA could. But it wasn't her.

He dismissed the PA with a 'Tell the woman that I am a Gujarati when she calls next. And connect me if she wants to talk with me.'

~

She did not call back that afternoon, nor for two more days. Her call came when he had almost forgotten about her. But he remembered her quickly when she greeted him in Gujarati: '*Kem chho*? (How are you?) I'm Shabana Meherali. I had called on Monday.'

'I got the message,' he said, in English. 'You were supposed to call back in the afternoon.'

'Sorry. I couldn't leave home again,' she said, still in Gujarati. 'I'm calling from a public telephone booth.'

What did that mean? That she did not have a telephone at home?

'I understand,' he mumbled.

'Which part of Gujarat do you come from?' she continued (in Gujarati).

'From Ahmedabad,' he said, slipping into Gujarati, 'but I was born and brought up in Bombay.'

'I was also born and brought up in Bombay,' she cried. 'I came to Pakistan only after my marriage. It was an arranged marriage,' she continued, as if in answer to a question. 'My father was in the garments exports business. Someone introduced him to my husband's father when he was visiting Dubai, and well, they arranged the marriage. We are Ismaili Khojas, Aga Khanis. You probably know some Khojas. There are many of us in Bombay.'

'Yes,' he said. 'There were several Khoja boys in school with me.'

'Which school did you go to?'

'The Cathedral,' he said. 'We lived in a flat near Haji Ali, not far from the school.'

'I loved to go to Haji Ali. It is a beautiful place.'

'I could see it from the window of my parents' bedroom,' he said. 'In fact our building is called Haji Ali View Tower.'

'How wonderful! Do your parents still live there?'

'My father does. My…' he checked himself. He was about to say that his mother was no more. That would have brought tears to his eyes. He thought of his mother every day, and could not forget that he had not been by her side the day she died. He had been attending some meeting in Delhi that had seemed important at that time. 'My father is a chartered accountant,' he said instead.

'We lived in Mahim,' she said. 'My mother still lives there, along with my brother and his family.'

'I had an aunt who lived in Mahim,' he said. 'In the Sindhi colony.'

'I know the place. I used to pass it on the way to the Mahim station. I thought only Sindhis lived there.'

'That's right. It was built on land earmarked for Hindu refugees from Karachi. My aunt was the only Gujarati living there. She had rented the place.'

A moment of silence followed. They seemed to have run out of subjects.

'So what can I do for you?' he broke the silence.

'Nothing,' she said. 'I just wanted to talk with you. I haven't talked with anybody in Gujarati in over fifteen years. My husband and his family speak Punjabi only. We live in a joint family.'

Another moment of silence followed. 'Well,' he said, 'it was nice talking with you…'

'One minute, one minute. May I call you again? I won't do it often, only when I am feeling very homesick for Gujarati.'

He did not know what to say.

'Please…'

'Certainly,' he said. 'Do call again.'

'Thank you.'

He mumbled something which he hoped meant 'mention not'.

'*Avjo*,' she said.

Gujaratis used the word 'avjo' to say goodbye, but the word meant more than that, he knew. It meant 'It was a pleasure to meet you. Please do come again'. He recalled how before they got married, his wife, who knew very little Gujarati, had greeted his parents, when they had gone to her place the first time, with 'avjo', instead of 'avo', which meant 'Please come in', causing much consternation and, a moment later, laughter.

'*Avjo*,' Shabana Meherali repeated.

'*Avjo*,' he said.

~

His hand stayed on the telephone for many moments after he had put it down. It had given him a strange pleasure to talk in Gujarati. Nobody in the High Commission, and nobody he had met in Pakistan, spoke the language. He missed it. Things must be much worse for her, with no hope of ever returning to people who spoke it.

~

She called again a few times in the months that followed. He learnt more about her. She was thirty-three years of age, so a year older than him. Her husband sold car spare parts. His shop, Meherali Automobiles, was in the mall, the main street in Rawalpindi. For years after their marriage they had no child. In desperation she had written to the Aga Khan for his blessings. A year later, she had a son. The son was five years old now. He was not always in good health, and stammered a bit, but he was the dearest boy in the world.

Her father was no more. She had not been able to go to Bombay for his funeral because the two countries were at war with each other at the time. Nobody was allowed to go to India.

She missed her mother. She hardly ever spoke to her on the phone though. Her husband's people did not like her making a trunk call to India—though there were two telephones in the house. Moreover the lines to Bombay were almost always down. But she wrote to her every week.

'Tell me about your family,' she asked.

He told her. His wife was a Bengali, named Ansuya. She was in the Indian Administrative Service. They had met during their training in Mussoorie. They had two children, a girl and a boy. She had stayed on in Delhi because of the children's education.

'And your parents, do they live alone?'

His mother had passed away two years back, he steeled himself and said, but he had a younger brother, who lived with their father. The brother was also a CA and worked in the father's firm.

~

Then one day she asked him if she could meet him in his office. 'Next Tuesday is Raksha Bandhan Day. I used to tie a rakhi on my brother's wrist on this day every year when we were young. May I tie one on your wrist?'

'Er…' He knew that the rakhi, a simple thread, linked two people as brother and sister for life.

'Please…'

'Certainly,' he said.

~

She was thinner than he had expected, and pale, and much flustered.

'There is a huge crowd of people outside,' she said, as he offered her a sofa chair.

He told her they were visa seekers.

'So many?'

He told her about the closure of the Indian Consulate in Karachi.

'I feel sorry for the poor people. I suppose there must also be a crowd of Hindu visa seekers outside the Pakistani High Commission in Delhi every day?'

'Er…there is a crowd, but not of Hindus. There are very few Hindus left in Pakistan. Most of them are poor people, living in the countryside in Sindh. They don't have relatives in India. So the crowd outside the Pakistani High Commission in Delhi consists of Muslims wishing to meet their relatives, the muhajirs, in Pakistan. Under the Indo-Pak visa agreement, only people who have relatives in the other country are entitled to visit it… Would you care for some tea?' he asked. 'Or a soft drink?'

'Tea please.'

'Good. I have some excellent tea from Assam. It is better than Darjeeling tea. Tea is an acquired taste, of course, but I do think that the best of Assam can beat the best of Darjeeling any day.'

She was still thinking about the crowd outside. 'So the Partition has divided Muslims only,' she said suddenly.

'Something like that,' he murmured and asked his PA to get them tea and biscuits.

As they waited for the tea, she brought out a coloured thread and tied it on his wrist. 'May you always remain in good health,' she gave him the customary blessing. 'And may all your wishes come true.'

He gave her an Indian shawl as a gift.

She showed him a photograph of her son. He had a finely shaped head but his eyes looked sad and there were shadows beneath them, as if he had just come out of a long illness.

'He is handsome,' he said, handing back the photograph. 'What is his name?'

'Karim,' she beamed and put the photograph back in her purse. 'Do you have a photograph of your wife and children?'

He picked up a framed photograph from his table and handed it to her.

'They are sweet,' she said after studying the photograph for a few moments. 'And Ansuya is lovely… Whose is the other photograph?'

'My parents.' He handed her the photograph. 'It was taken about a year before my mother passed away.'

She gazed at the photograph for a long time. 'You look like your mother,' she said by and by, handing back the photograph.

'But for my big nose. I have my father to thank for that.' She laughed.

'Who looks after him?' she asked.

'Servants. But really my brother.'

'Is your brother married?'

'Not yet.'

'A good thing,' she cried. 'My brother was a loving son before he got married. Not now. He is just too scared of his wife. And she is a tyrant,' she continued. 'I have often asked him to look after mother properly…'

He kept quiet.

'Every day I feel like going to Bombay to look after her. Once I even got a visa application form from the Indian High Commission… But I can't leave my son,' she said.

Tea arrived. They spoke about other things then: a recent Bombay film; an old Gujarati play which, they learnt to their delight, both of them had seen; a Navratri garba dance that (dressed in a sari) she had gone to once; bhelpuri at Juhu; walking on Marine Drive; their favourite restaurants for Gujarati thalis…

'In my view, the Chetna thali is the best,' he said.

'I prefer Purohit's,' she said. 'It gives you value for money.' They laughed.

'Oh, what time is it?' she asked suddenly. 'Twelve? I should be going,' she rose.

He escorted her to the gate. The crowd outside seemed to have increased. 'I feel sad for the people,' she said once more. 'Can't you do something to give them the visas faster?'

'I wish we could; but without the Consulate in Karachi…' He left the rest unsaid.

And out of the blue she said, 'I'll write to the Aga Khan for his blessings—that the Consulate in Karachi be reopened soon.'

'That would be nice,' he said.

'He is a very good man. Very caring. Shall I tell you a secret? When I was in school, I used to dream that some day he would come to our school, see me and ask me to marry him. He wasn't married in those days… Alas, a beautiful girl got him first,' she laughed.

'*His* loss,' he said gallantly.

'Thank you,' she said, 'brother,' she added, patting the thread on his wrist.

He felt a sudden urge to tell her that she really was

beautiful, and wonderful, and lovable, the sister that he always wanted; and that he would speak to her husband and in-laws to cast aside their prism of prejudices and see her as she really was, and treat her and her son well; that he too hoped that the Aga Khan will succeed in persuading the Government of Pakistan to let India reopen its Consulate in Karachi—and maybe someday in removing the poison that has seeped into so many millions of hearts after the partition of India.

'How are you going back, Shabana?' he asked instead.

'I will catch a bus from Jinnah Market,' she said. 'It is a short walk from here.'

Should he offer to drop her? His security guards were staring at him—and her. So were also a couple of Pakistani policemen from across the street. He mumbled, 'Well, call me anytime you feel like it.'

'*Avjo*,' she smiled and said.

'*Avjo*.'

~

He wondered, as he returned to his room, if the Aga Khan would really do anything to get the Indian Consulate in Karachi reopened. He might. That was the only way that divided Aga Khani Khoja families—*his* people—could meet without going through the long, messy and uncertain route of Islamabad. Suddenly the irony of the whole thing struck him. It was the grandfather of the present Aga Khan, the old Aga Khan, who had presided over the whole business of separating Muslims from Hindus by founding the All-India Muslim League back in 1906 and encouraging the British to partition Bengal. That had led, almost inevitably, to the partition of the whole country forty years later.

~

Then one day he heard that there were anti-Shi‘a riots in Lahore and some other places in the Punjab. The riots had been quickly suppressed, along with news of exactly what had happened and how many people had been killed but, he sensed, not before sending a shiver down the spine of every Shi‘a in Pakistan. This was not the first time that there were riots against Shi‘as in Pakistan, nor would it be the last time. Almost from the start—and certainly after the massacre, years back, of hundreds of Shi‘as in Khairpur—the Shi‘as of Pakistan had been singled out by Sunnis as being ‘the other’, deserving punishment. To be sure, Sunnis everywhere in the world disliked Shi‘as, but it seemed incredible that there should be dislike of them in Pakistan. Shi‘as had been at the forefront of the struggle for Pakistan. The Father of the Nation, Jinnah himself was a Shi‘a, that too born a Khoja. The man must be turning in his grave.

He wondered if Shabana was safe. Should he telephone her and ask?... The call could cause problems for her. Apart from everything else, her in-laws must fear any attention drawn to them at a time like this. And a telephone call from him would do worse than that; it would focus the spotlight on them. He decided not to make the call. A few more days passed. Then he got a call from her.

She did not mention her name. ‘*Hoon chhoon* (It is me),’ she spoke rapidly. ‘I just want you to know that we are all right. It was bad for some other people, but we are safe.’

'I was worried…'

'I knew you would be. But I must put down the phone now.'

~

A few more weeks passed. The riots became a distant memory, replaced by news of troubles elsewhere: the killing of some Hazaras (who were also Shi'as) in Quetta, a suicide bomb attack in a Peshawar bazaar, clashes between Pathans and Muhajirs in Karachi… Then one day she called. It was an SOS.

'My mother has had a heart attack. She is in hospital. I must rush to Bombay. I need visas for India.'

'Please fill in the application form—do you still have it?'

'Yes.'

'Excellent. Just fill it up and mail it to me quickly,' he said. 'I will forward it right away to Delhi with a request to give you visas on an urgent basis.'

'Can't *you* give me the visas?'

'I'm sorry I can't. Only Delhi can.'

'How long will Delhi take?'

'It is difficult to say…'

'But my mother has had a heart attack,' she repeated. 'She is in hospital!' she cried.

'I understand. And I promise I will try my best. Just send me the application form. If you have any difficulty with any of the columns of the form, don't worry. I will fill those in. Call me.'

The visa application form had sixty-three columns. He

was sure that it had been devised by a policeman who suspected that every Pakistani who wanted to come to India was a spy or smuggler or worse. Even the clerks in the visa section had difficulty advising applicants how to fill in the form. Repeatedly the High Commission had asked Delhi to simplify it. Delhi had refused to remove a single column from it.

She sent him a half-filled but signed form and telephoned him for the remaining columns. He filled in the missing information while she answered his questions. Then he rushed the form to Delhi by the next diplomatic bag, followed that up with a telex message to the Deputy Secretary concerned, and finally tried to speak to him on the telephone. The fellow's phone was always engaged—or maybe the lines were bad. He sent him another telex message and tried to telephone him again, and again…

She called him every day. Her anxiety grew when she received a letter from her mother conveying that she had been brought home from hospital but was more or less bedridden. '*Koine kyare buddha ne thavoon joiye* (Nobody should ever become old),' she had scribbled in the end. 'One becomes a burden on people.'

He had no fresh news to give her. Then one day he finally got the Deputy Secretary in Delhi on the line. The DS said that he would check up and let him know; there were so many visa applications. The man never called back. When finally, a week later, he got him on the phone again, the man asked him if he had any idea who this S. Meherali was. 'His name is in bold letters in our blacklist of residents of Karachi!'

'The Meherali I am talking about lives in Rawalpindi and is a woman,' Rahul said dryly.

'Are you sure?'

'Yes. I have met her.'

'And she is a woman…'

Rahul struggled to keep calm. Was this some kind of joke? No, it was probably Delhi's way of investigating things thoroughly. He said in an even voice, 'Yes.'

'Hmm. We will look into the case again.'

'Please do. Shall I call you tomorrow?'

'Don't take the trouble. I'll call you.'

To his surprise, the man called back, though four days later. 'We have reconsidered her case. We can grant her the visas but her form has been filled up in two different hands, as if by two different people.'

'That's right. I helped her fill it in.'

'That was er…irregular. But never mind. Just send us a fresh form, filled in only by her and we will grant her the visas.'

He called her. Some other woman picked up the phone and, when he introduced himself and asked for Shabana Meherali, said that she had gone to the jamaatkhana to pray for her mother's soul. Her mother had passed away the previous night in Bombay. No, the woman replied when he asked, Shabana does not need the Indian visas now. She will not be going to Bombay.

~

A month passed. Then a few more months. She never called him back. But he received a rakhi from her on Raksha

Bandhan Day the next year, and every year thereafter, c/o the High Commission of India in Islamabad, to be redirected to him wherever he was, along with a card that read…

> *May you always remain in good health. May all your wishes come true.*
>
> S.M.

…till one year, almost a decade later, when there were anti-Shi'a riots in Lahore and elsewhere in Pakistan. News of exactly what had happened was quickly suppressed but it was believed that many people, including scores of women and children, were killed in the riots.

Janaki

Janaki, as I'm sure you know, is another name of Sita, Lord Ram's beautiful, beloved and chaste wife, a role model for wives for all time to come.

It is also the name of our maid. Is she also beautiful? Alas, yes. Is she beloved? Yes, in fact very beloved. Chaste? I don't know what to say. You decide. But wait till you have heard the whole story.

~

It all began the morning my wife got a telephone call from Meena, wife of Major-General (retd) 'Tippy' Sharma, the hero of the Kargil war. They have known each other since they were both in KG in a nursery school in Jorbagh. They were both leading members of a kitty group in Vasant Vihar, which has probably the most active kitty groups in all of Delhi. Meena was the first person that she had called when our search for a maid had started almost a month back.

'Are you still looking for a maid, Renu?' she asked.

'Yes,' Renu sighed. 'Everybody I have interviewed is so substandard. Why, have you found someone?'

'Yes.'

'Who?'

'Janaki.'

'Janaki who?'

'My maid. You saw her when you came to my house for rummy on Diwali. Remember?'

'*Your* maid? You are giving me *your* maid?'

'Yes.'

'But you said that she is an outstanding cook…'

'Yes.'

'…that she even knows manicure and pedicure, and can dye hair to perfection…'

'Yes.'

'…and gives you a wonderful massage.'

'Yes.'

'Then why are you letting her go?' Renu came to the point.

'What are friends for,' Meena said, 'if they don't help each other in times of need?'

'That is true…' Renu murmured. A few moments passed. I could read her mind. The offer was too good to be true. There had to be a catch somewhere. What could it be?

'So, do you want her or not?' Meena asked, her voice acquiring a tinge of impatience.

'Say yes,' I whispered to Renu.

'Of course I want her, Meena,' Renu said. 'I was just looking for the right words with which to thank you. Please give her my address. Ask her to come right away.'

~

Perhaps I should tell you here why we were in search of a maid. A month back I had received orders transferring me to Rome as India's ambassador to Italy. To say that I was pleased with the orders is to say the obvious. All my life I have been interested in antiquity, Indian as well as European. I did my BA *and* MA in history. The thesis I wrote for my PhD was on the representation of beauty in ancient Sanskrit literature—I know Sanskrit. I know Latin too. But life is unfair. You never get the postings you deserve. I had got only (historically) uninteresting postings in my three decades in the Indian Foreign Service. And frankly, with less than four years to go before retiring from service, I had given up all hopes of ever being sent to a decent place. And along had come this miracle: transfer to a country of great antiquity, with an awe-inspiring, many-layered past that few countries in the world can boast of. The whole night after getting the orders I had dreamt of exploring Rome and other old cities of that ancient land, interacting with Italian academicians and others and, well, making a name for myself as a scholar of Indian culture and ancient Sanskrit literature, especially the great Hindu epics, *Ramayana* and *Mahabharata*.

The next morning, however, had brought me down to earth with a thud. Our maid, named Sita by a strange coincidence, had said no to coming with us to Rome. She was getting married shortly, she said, and her duty was to stay with her husband, keep his home, take care of him, cook for him... All very noble and quite what it should be, I admit, but my first thought had been quite selfish, that her resolve had left us with no one to stay with *us*, to keep *our* home…above all, to cook for us. For Renu, a wonderful woman in many ways, cannot cook. Indeed, it is one of her boasts that she has never entered a kitchen. She has always been lucky with her cooks.

There was nothing to be done about it, of course, save to find another maid, and I had said so to Renu. Fortunately, there were still six weeks to go before our departure. And I must say to Renu's credit that she had left no stone unturned to find a maid. All to no avail. 'I can't believe,' she had said to me at the end of a month of the search, 'that in this whole city of maybe a million jobless people, there is not one good maid we can take with us to Rome.' To cut a long story short, we had begun to get desperate. Renu had even lowered our requirements to 'a cook, male or female', assuring me that we could do the washing and the rest of the housework 'ourselves'. That meant mainly me, I knew, but I had readily agreed to it. Any delay in our departure and the opportunity of going to Rome could slip out of my hands. There were far too many fellows waiting in the wings to grab the place.

That was when Meena had called and offered us Janaki.

~

'Do you think there is something wrong with her?' my wife asked me as we waited for the maid. 'I have known Meena all my life. She is the last person in the world to let go a maid to help a friend.'

'Perhaps you are judging Meena too harshly,' I said. 'There is a spark of goodness in all of us. As the story of sage Valmiki in *Ramayana* shows, that spark—'

'I am not talking about Meena,' she cut me short. 'I'm talking about the maid, Janaki. Could she have done something wrong?'

'Like what?'

'Stolen something; broken something; brought her boyfriend to the house... There are hundreds of ways in which a maid can do wrong.'

'Hmm,' I reflected for a moment. 'Not with a name like Janaki,' I finally said. 'Names matter, you see. They give us an image we strive to live up to. And the name Janaki, associated as it is with the place of Sita's birth, gives a certain depth to the character of Sita, an extra dimension to it, a special fragrance of integrity and dependability. I have explained this in some detail in my tract on *The names in Hindu Epics* published by the Indian Council of Cultural Relations last January. If you wish to read it, I have a copy of it saved on my hard—'

'Later,' Renu said, and called our daughter in Singapore. Bidya had stood first in MA (Psychology) in JNU, and was now working as Assistant Professor in NUS. Her husband, who too wore thick glasses, was head of some NGO there. Mother and daughter spoke to each other every day, thanks to Skype.

'Is she beautiful?' Bidya asked after listening to a blow-by-blow account, and some more, of Meena's offer. 'For that could be the problem.'

~

'Is she beautiful?' my wife asked me, in Bengali, when the maid turned up.

I looked at the girl. Actually I had been doing nothing else since the moment she had glided in through the door, for she had brought rushing to my mind the description of a maiden, from head to toe, in a third-century Sanskrit play that I had read but recently: with the eyes of a doe; neck of a gazelle; breasts like lotus buds bursting to see the world; voice of a koel (songbird); waist of a young lioness; walk of a swan; thighs of…

'Well,' my wife repeated impatiently. 'Is she beautiful?'

I averted my eyes and said, 'Not my type.'

'Who is asking you if she is your type? Is she beautiful?'

'No!' I lied.

'Are you sure?'

'Yes. But if you want me to look at her again, I—'

'That will not be necessary,' Renu snapped, and turning to the maid, asked, 'How old are you?'

'Almost twenty, memsahib,' said Janaki, looking up with her doe's slightly frightened eyes.

'Do you have a birth certificate? A school-leaving certificate?…'

'Yes, memsahib,' she fished out a school-leaving certificate from her bag and handed it to Renu. Renu passed it to me to examine and continued.

'How come you are still not married?'

'My father doesn't have the money for the dowry, memsahib.'

'Hmm… Where do you come from?'

'From the hills, memsahib.'

That could mean any place in the Himalayas from the Pakistan to the Bangladesh border. 'From where, exactly?' Renuka asked.

'From Kumaon, memsahib.'

Women of Kumaon, I reminded Renu (in Bengali) had the reputation of being both dependable as well as scrupulously honest. 'Moreover, she was born on the 8th of September,' I continued, 'and is therefore a Virgo. Virgos are also very hard-working, practically workaholics,' I added, 'apart from being, er…virtuous.'

'Hmm.' But Renu had still one last question. 'Why do you want to leave Meena-memsahib and come with us?'

'Memsahib asked me to, memsahib.'

That was not an entirely satisfactory answer but we hired her. We did not carry out a police verification of her either. That takes months. In any case, no police verification of Janaki could have been of any use—for the simple reason that no policeman could have ever known a case like Janaki's, I mean what she did later. But we got an undertaking in writing from her that she would stay with us for the duration of our stay in Rome. In return we gave her an assurance that at the end of every month half her salary would be credited to her bank account in Delhi, the other half to her bank account in Rome.

We had to show her as twenty-one years of age in her passport. The Government had just made that the minimum age for all maids going abroad. We also had to describe her as 'Technical domestic assistant' in the Italian visa application form. Lately, several European governments had begun to object to foreign diplomats bringing domestic servants with them. They said it amounted to slavery. (There was no point in reminding them that all European diplomats in Delhi employed platoons of servants.) Calling Janaki 'Technical domestic assistant' smoothened her passage to Italy.

There was no time to test her cooking skills. We had to wind up the household. But Renu did ask her to make aloo-parathas for us once. They were out of this world. One did not need even dahi or pickles to relish them. Two days before our departure, the girl also trimmed Renu's hair, dyed it, trimmed also her finger and toe nails, painted them to perfection and gave her a massage.

'How was the massage?' I asked her later.

'Excellent. The girl has magic in her hands. Whatever could have made Meena let her go?'

~

I got the answer to the question just two days later, at the Indira Gandhi Airport. We had completed the immigration and security formalities; Renu was doing some last-minute shopping in a duty-free shop; Janaki was waiting at the departure gate, guarding our handbags. I went to Men's—and ran into Brigadier (retd) Verma on my way out.

'Hi there!' he began.

'Oh hello, Brigadier!' I said.

Brigadier Verma and I shared an interest in common: early morning walks. Often, after the walk, we sat down in a café for a cup of tea and gossip. Mostly he talked; I listened. He was a coursemate of General Sharma so the talk often turned to him.

'Leaving for Rome?' he asked.

'Yes. But I'll be back for our walks in three years. And you? Where are you headed?'

'Nepal, for a bit of trekking... Heard the latest about Sharma, our war hero?'

'What about him?'

'He is under house arrest.'

'What?'

'Meena's orders.'

'Oh!'

'Apparently she found him hugging their maid's shoulder, giving her a five-hundred-rupee note, and saying: "If you ever need anything, just let me know."' The Brigadier laughed.

My mouth went dry. 'I see...' I managed to mumble. Once or twice I myself had felt the urge to put a fatherly arm round the girl's shoulders and say something comforting to her. Luckily, I had remembered sage Vidur's centuries-old wise words of caution against such urges, and had suppressed it.

'Actually, Meena went for the maid first, wishing to pull her hair out,' the Brigadier continued. 'And you know what the maid did? She stared coolly into Meena's eyes and said that if she so much as touched her, she would tell the whole world *everything*,' the Brigadier laughed again, 'yes, *everything*, whatever that means. Then, as Meena stopped in her tracks, the girl added that she would not say anything to anybody if she got a month's severance pay and a recommendation for another job. The recommendation must say that she is honest and hard-working, and has a good moral character. Meena glared at her as if she wanted to throttle her, but in the end good sense prevailed. She paid her the money and palmed her off on some female in her kitty gang. And then put our hero in the cooler.'

'Sad!' I murmured, 'But I must not miss my flight.' Somehow, I managed to find my way back to Renu, and thence into the First Class cabin of our plane. Janaki was travelling by the Economy class.

~

'What are you thinking about?' Renu asked me when we were probably flying over Iran. 'You haven't said a word since we left Delhi.'

'Nothing,' I said. That was true. I was thinking of nothing. I did not know what to think. We were already launched on a voyage into the unknown with a blackmailer as our maid. Was she also a temptress? Brigadier Verma's account of General Sharma's hugging her was not clear on this point. But young maidens, as described so well in a poem by Raja Bharthari two thousand years ago, can tempt a man without saying a word... Should I share my fears, my nameless dread, with Renu? I decided against the idea. It could only make matters worse. 'Nothing,' I repeated.

'Suit yourself,' she shrugged, and ordered herself another glass of wine.

~

The Indian embassy in Rome was a middle-sized mission, with local employees outnumbering the ones from India. Not all the locals were Italian. Many were Indian, several of them, alas, young men with questionable right to live and work in Italy. Three or four of them (a Bengali, a Sikh, a Haryanvi, and an Odia) I suspected, had no right at all. The Bengali worked as a sort of multipurpose handyman for the

Residence as well as the office. The other three worked at the Residence only, two of them as security guards and the Sikh as the gardener. My predecessor had employed them, I was told, because he had found it impossible to recruit Italians on the poor salaries sanctioned by Delhi; and they had taken the job because working for the embassy was the safest way for them to stay on in Italy till something better came along. In addition to these, two Italians worked directly under me at the Residence. They were my chauffeur, a young man called Antonio, and Maria, a middle-aged caretaker.

~

I had dozed fitfully in the plane, but by the time we came out of the airport in Rome, I had almost forgotten about the danger that Janaki posed. Then I saw Antonio's jaw drop when he saw her and alarm bells started ringing in my head. Mercifully, Janaki travelled in the car with the bags, not with us, but four more jaws dropped when we reached the Residence, one Bengali, one Sikh, one Haryanvi and one Odia. Strangely, Renu noticed nothing, or maybe she thought that the jaws had dropped for her. (In her talk with Bidya that evening, she said that her Benarsi sari was a great hit.) But Maria noticed. She welcomed us with typical Italian cheer, but Janaki with her eyes narrowed, lips pursed and jaw firmly shut. Janaki responded by entering the house with her head suitably bowed. But a smile hovered on her lips. I did not like the smile. It made me feel that I had stepped into some sort of jungle. Behind every bush, round every corner, lurked danger. What should I do?

I did what the *Bhagwat Gita* suggests. I immersed myself in work, reading up every important file in the embassy on Italy and our relations with it, calling on important people, sending my first dispatches to Delhi, drawing up plans to visit Florence, Venice, Naples… Renu too settled down quickly to our new life, thanks largely to—I must give the devil her due—Janaki. Janaki bought the groceries and other daily necessities for the house, cooked for us, cleaned for us, tidied up for us, and yet finished in four hours what others would take eight hours to do. Antonio drove her to the shops and back and helped her in the house whenever he was free, though that was not his job. He also gave her an iPhone, saying that he had bought a new one and had no use for the old one—and taught her how to use it. As to how they conversed with each other, I have no idea. She knew no Italian and very little English; Antonio knew no Hindi. Soon, however, she was at the iPhone for several hours every day, teaching herself English and God alone knows what else.

Sunday was her day off. She spent the first Sunday washing, ironing and hanging up the curtains, and the second in making our garden more presentable. The third Sunday we had a housewarming party in the garden, a wine and cheese affair. Almost five hundred people attended it, including, in a rare honour to India, Italy's Prime Minister himself. The old man did not attend many parties. But the person to turn the most heads at the party, I noticed, was not he but Janaki, though (upon Maria's insistence) she had worn a white apron, like the other servers, and no makeup, so that she would not be mistaken for a guest.

Soon Janaki started going out on Sundays and receiving and making mysterious calls on the infernal iPhone that Antonio had given her. We had no idea where she went, whom she met, nor whom all she spoke to on the telephone. But she gave us no cause for complaint as far as her work was concerned. Her cooking was superb, her massage (so Renu told me) equally so and, wonder of wonders, she had a green thumb. Under her supervision, the garden turned into a joy to behold.

Months passed, during which I found myself getting busier and busier. Italian interest in an India fast emerging as an economic powerhouse was considerable, and it was growing by the day. Moreover, almost by definition, Italians were great lovers of culture. Renu and I were invited to so many parties that we hardly ever ate dinner at home, save when we ourselves hosted a party, which we did at the rate of four or five a month. Almost every week we had important visitors from India. They expected to be served Indian food. India and Italy signed seven economic and cultural agreements that year, a record.

Not all my interactions with the people of Italy were serious and businesslike. Many were not. An example?

At a party held in my honour in Pisa, a woman asked me if I would teach her how to wear a sari! (Renu replied before I could think of a proper answer: 'My husband is a wizard at removing the sari but, alas, knows nothing about how to put it on. Come, let me show it to you.' The general laughter that followed, I was told, could be heard in the street outside.)

One more example? An inebriated guest at a party in

Milan who, dragging by his hand his clearly mortified wife behind him, asked me whether it was true that once a woman had made love with a Sikh man, she would not be happy with anybody else. (Renu was not there to field the question, so I tried my diplomatic best. 'All I know,' I said, remembering a sentence from *Arthashastra*, the ancient Indian treatise on statecraft, 'is that people often say things they don't mean.')

Then there was this lady who had recently returned from a trip to India and who wanted to know where in Rome she could buy that utterly delicious Indian dish called chaprasi which is buttered on both sides and is a bit heavy on the stomach!

Virtually every two or three weeks I was invited to make a speech to a select gathering at some place or the other in Italy. My speech at the Perugia University on *The essence of Hinduism and Jesus Christ* was so well appreciated that translated extracts from it appeared in *Corriere dell'Umbria*, a local newspaper, and later in several other newspapers in Italy. My speech at Milan on the *Mahabharata, a moral tale* was so well received that the sale of that classic shot up in that city! Newspapers and magazines carried interviews of me. TV channels sought me out for my views every time India was in the news... My wife too was busy with an ever larger circle of friends. Months flew. I forgot the sword of Damocles hanging on our heads.

Then one morning the sword fell. Janaki told us that she was getting married.

'Oh!' Renu said. I said nothing. I knew that probably half a dozen fellows in the embassy alone were interested in her, but I had calmed myself into believing that there was safety in numbers. Janaki herself had given us not the slightest hint that she was interested in anyone. Now I wondered, as did Renu I was sure, about what would happen to us if she got married.

'To Antonio,' she added when neither of us said anything.

I should have guessed. The fellow was good-looking. And he had been wooing her for months.

She continued, 'We will go on a holiday to London for two weeks but I will return and continue working with you—for the present.'

We did not like her last three words but we began to breathe easier. By and by we even congratulated them and told them to have a good time in London.

~

I wish I could end the story here with 'And they lived happily ever after'. But they did not. So read on…

They could not go to London for their honeymoon. There was some problem with her (Indian) passport, they said. They decided to go there after she had become an Italian citizen and acquired an Italian passport (which would take just a couple of months, she was told) and in the meantime to go to Venice instead. To our great relief, they returned in four days. She continued working with us, exactly as before, as if she had not married at all. And Antonio kept helping her…

…till the day she got her Italian citizenship and passport. I was in the house when the mail came. Renu and

I looked at each other as she tore open the thick envelope and pulled out the passport.

Would she and Antonio go on that trip to London now? The days when she had gone to Venice had been days of much hardship for us. Two weeks of her absence would be murder. But they had every right to go on the trip. We might as well move into a hotel, I reflected. But then what about the dinner that I had to host for a parliamentary delegation from Delhi visiting us that week? They would expect me to serve them Indian food.

She did not go to London. After a long walk in the garden, she told us that it was her duty to help with the dinner for the MPs. I felt so overwhelmed by her generous decision that I could have given her a hug that moment, and followed it up with a large lira note. I didn't do anything of the kind, of course. Renu was right there. So we had that party in the house, and the MPs went back happy to Delhi.

A week of peace passed. It was shattered by a bolt from the blue. Janaki told us that she and Antonio had got divorced—by mutual consent. Neither of them had said anything, not even given us the slightest hint, to prepare us for the news. And now neither would tell us why they had got divorced. Antonio only requested that he be shifted to another duty—driving one of the staff cars—so that he would be away from the Residence. Naturally I did so.

~

It was a sad ending—both of us liked Antonio—but, as we were soon to learn, not the last ending. For another week later, Janaki told us that she was getting married again—to Harry.

'Harry who?' we cried.

'Harbans Singh.'

'The gardener?' we asked, astonished. She nodded.

'You are spoilt goods!' Renu cried angrily. 'Or doesn't he know that you were married to Antonio?'

Janaki turned red, but soon regained her composure and said, 'He knows. And just for your information, I am...' she brought out her iPhone, pressed a few buttons with the dexterity that only the young have, stopped when she had found what she was looking for, and turned the screen for Renu to read. It read *Virgo intacta*. And before we could say anything, she turned her back and flounced out of the room.

Renu asked me to check up with Antonio if that was true. I said I could not possibly ask him something like that; it was too private a matter. Renu said that in that case she would ask him. I said all right, I will ask him.

I asked him.

'I guess she is,' he replied. 'I mean, I never touched her. She would not allow me to. She said that under some vow she had taken, she had to wait for six months after the marriage to consummate it.'

'And you believed her?' I cried.

He nodded. 'I was a fool.'

'She used you!' I fumed.

'I suppose so.'

'Then why did you consent to the divorce?' I continued, unable to stop now. 'You could have challenged the suit.'

'To be honest, I did think of that, sir. But she said that in that case she would file for a divorce on the ground that I, er...could not fulfil my husbandly duty.'

'What!'

'So you see, sir, I had no choice.'

I told Renu what Antonio had told me. 'It is not our business,' I said in the end, 'what she does in her private life. You see, so long as she continues working with us, we...'

'Oh!' Renu exclaimed. And she summoned Janaki and told her that she trusted that like when she had got married the first time, she would continue working for us this time too.

And you know what the maid said? She said that she would very much like to, but after marriage it would be her duty to stay with her husband, keep his home, cook for him, wait on him hand and foot...

~

Renu narrated the story to Bidya on Skype that evening and asked, 'Should we hold the girl by the contract she has signed with us?'

'Er... I wouldn't advise it,' Bidya said after a moment. 'It could open up a Pandora's box.'

'Oh! Then what should we do?' Renu wailed.

'You could...' Bidya hesitated.

'Yes?'

'...learn some cooking, mummy,' Bidya said gently.

Benghazi

There are not many Indians in Benghazi now: a few doctors, a few nurses, a few labourers… Time was, not too long ago, when thousands of Indians worked there—doctors and nurses of course, but also engineers, professors, teachers, consultants, contractors, builders, accountants… A fair-sized Indian Consulate looked after their passport, visa and other consular needs. At the time the events described in this tale took place, the Consulate was headed by one Shri Hariprasad Tripathi, a good and kind man but, sadly, also a lonely man, having lost his wife in a botched operation in a Delhi hospital a few years back. 'Ours was a happy marriage,' he said whenever he spoke of his wife or of marriage generally. 'We always made an effort to adjust. Marriage is like a stringed bow, you see. For it to work well, both the bow and the string need to bend—in other words, to adjust. Oh yes, adjustment is the key to a happy marriage.'

As it should happen, he had occasion to utter the wise words the very day he arrived in Benghazi, for he was invited to say a few words to the guests at an Indian wedding reception. The speech was well received, he thought, but later, after he got to know the Indian community a little better, he wondered if the people had really understood it. They were a young lot, mostly in their twenties or thirties, and therefore, almost by definition, with a limited understanding of life. That was also evident from the answers they gave him whenever he asked any of them—husbands or wives—if they were happy in Benghazi. The husbands laughed and said of course they were happy there, for their wives could not throw away their hard-earned money there. The place had few real shops, only government-run souks that sold just the basic necessities, never things like jewellery or perfumes or whatnot. The wives too laughed and said that they were happy in Benghazi, for their mothers-in-law could not get at them there. Libyan rules did not allow foreigners to bring to Libya members of their extended families.

But this tale is not about Shri Tripathi, nor about the Indian community in Benghazi, not really…

~

One morning, when the eastern sky was just turning light—Shri Tripathi was an early riser—and the birds in the large juniper tree outside his bedroom window were chirruping their small, blessed hearts out, there was a knock on his door. It was a young woman. Her lower lip was swollen with caked blood. Her right temple was a mess of hair and blood. Her eyes were red. Her cheeks showed traces of tears. Her sari was crumpled and dusty. Was she pregnant? Probably, he thought, quickly looking away.

'May I have a glass of water, please?' she stammered. 'I've spent the whole night in the park.'

He asked his servant to quickly bring a jug of cold water and invited her in.

'You are hurt, beti,' he said after she had gulped down two glasses of water. 'Have you had an accident?'

She looked away, sudden tears brimming her eyes.

He wondered what he should say next. 'Would you like to wash up, beti?' he suggested after a moment. 'The washroom is over there,' he pointed, 'the second door on the left. There is, er…a bottle of Dettol in the closet. We will have tea afterwards.'

She went to the washroom. He asked the servant to bring a pot of tea and something to eat, quickly, even if just bread and butter. Then he sat down by a table in the verandah and waited for her. Who could she be? And why had she spent the night in the park?… The servant brought the tea-things and placed them on the table… What could have caused those injuries on her? Could she have been…? He hoped not. It would be awful if…

She came out of the washroom before he could think further. He looked at her wounds furtively, decided that they did not require immediate medical attention and cut her a slice of bread. She grabbed it before he could finish buttering it and ate it ravenously. He buttered a second slice faster, handed it to her and made her a cup of tea. She winced from pain when the cup touched her lips but she continued to sip it, carefully now.

'I've not had an accident,' she murmured by and by.

He waited.

'I… Last evening… My name is Meera,' she said when she began next. 'I'm from Bulandshahr, daughter of Pandit

Shivraj Mishra. Everybody in Bulandshahr knows him—he is a Sanskrit scholar. He has retired now. I am—I was—his favourite…' Her voice broke.

'I too adored him,' she resumed after a moment. 'Even when I was a child, I used to tell everybody that I wanted to become a teacher—like him. I did not change my mind when I became older. I became a teacher and even taught for a year in the local KVS…'

'Sanskrit?' he asked when she did not say anything more.

'No. Maths.'

'A most useful subject,' he mumbled.

'Hmm… But then I met my husband on Facebook—he was also from Bulandshahr, though he was working for a Korean company in Benghazi—and after some months, agreed to marry him…' She fell silent again.

'I see,' Shri Tripathi said.

'My father said no to my marrying him. (My husband is a Kayastha.) I reminded my father that he had always said that the caste system was wrong. He said that he stood by what he had said about the caste system—it *was* wrong. But now we were talking about marriage, which was a serious matter. We argued for many days. But that only made matters worse. Finally, he said angrily that I had to choose between the family and marrying outside the caste. My mother too did not support me, saying that nobody would marry my younger sister if I married a Kayastha… I married him nevertheless, thinking that they would have a change of heart once I had a child, and came away with my husband to Benghazi. I wrote several letters to my parents after that. I got no reply from them, only one brief letter from my sister that father had taken a vow never to see my face again. That upset me but I still hoped that things would work out once I had a child… About a year after our marriage, I had a daughter, Rupa. She is the most beautiful baby in the world…' Her voice broke again.

'Er… Some more tea?' Shri Tripathi asked.

She shook her head. 'Rupa is a year and six months old. She is very bright. She can speak a lot of words already…'

Shri Tripathi smiled.

'We could not go to India last year—my husband did not get leave. We were planning to go this year. But about six months back, my mother-in-law joined us—the company that my husband works for had helped to obtain visas for her—and everything changed. Within hours of her coming, she started picking on me. It began with her criticizing my cooking but soon spread to whatever I was doing, even when I did things exactly as she said I should do them. It was awful, just like on TV. I never answered back. I did not answer back even when she started criticizing me for not just what I was doing but also for what I was. Even my not answering back annoyed her. "Have you stuffed your mouth with moong," she said, "that you can't talk?" Still, I kept quiet… But then she started picking on Rupa.

'"A daughter!" she said. "That's all you are capable of producing. At your age, I had already produced three sons—and no daughter.

'"Rupa! What a name for someone so dark. Kali, that's what you should have named her. Kali. Black."

'"What's the matter with the girl?" she cried when Rupa began to refuse to go to her. "Is something wrong with her? There *is* something wrong with her. Look at her eyes. They are not normal."

'One day I exploded. "Rupa is no darker than her father," I cried. "In any case, why are you saying these awful things about her? What harm has she done you? She is just a baby… Is it her fault that she is a girl? Is it my fault that I am a woman? Is it your fault that you are a woman? You too are a woman, you know."

'She changed the subject. "If my son had married anybody else," she said, "he would have got a dowry of one crore at least. What did you bring? Nothing! Zero."

'I fought back. "I was earning good money as a teacher in Bulandshahr. I can teach here too. It is your son who is stopping me from teaching…"

'But my arguing back did not help. In fact, she started to pull my husband into our battles.

'"This is what you get for marrying a Brahmin girl," she said.

'"This is what you get for marrying an educated girl," she added.

'"This is what you get for marrying a shameless girl, always answering back," she continued. "Oh, send me back to India. I don't want to live in this house a day more."

'My husband did not say anything at those times, just sat there, scowling, although he knew that I was right. Then suddenly one day he flared up, taking *her* side.

'"Ma wanted ghee on her chapati," he said. "Why have you given her a dry chapati?"

'"And it is stone cold," my mother-in-law added.

'"It is not cold, ma," I said, addressing her. "I took it out of the food warmer only ten seconds back. And the bowl of ghee is right next to you on the table..."

'And he slapped me. Just like that. I almost fell off the chair. Stunned, I left the table and went to the bedroom. He came to me an hour later, mumbled a sorry and... soon...proceeded to...touch me. I told him that I didn't want it. He didn't stop. I wept through it. He fell asleep immediately after it. I kept weeping.'

'My mother-in-law resumed the nagging the next morning and continued it through the day. The evening ended again in a fight, with him taking her side, though this time he did not slap me. Soon this became a pattern. Almost every day we had fights. Some evenings he beat me. Some nights he...forced me—which was worse than the beating. I'm pregnant again. I didn't want to have another child so soon. And Rupa has stopped smiling...' She broke down again.

Shri Tripathi cleared his throat to say that sometimes these things happened in marriage.

'They should not happen,' she cried.

'Er... True,' he mumbled.

She resumed after a moment. 'Things came to a head about a week back, when my husband's younger brother joined us—my husband has got him too a job in his company. I had hoped that things would improve with him in the house, but they only got worse...

'Last evening, before my husband had returned from work, and I was feeding Rupa milk, my mother-in-law said, "No amount of milk is going to make her fair," and I cried, "Fair, fair, fair… Can't you see anything else in her? Have you become so blind that…?" And suddenly he—my brother-in-law—slapped me, sending the milk bottle flying and Rupa crying. I lost my temper then and started screaming at him, not realizing that my husband had just come into the house. "How dare you slap me? You are my devar, my husband's *younger* brother. I am your bhabhi. What right do you have to raise your hand against me? What shastra allows that? Did Laxman ever raise his hand against Sita? And if your hand is that itchy, why don't you get married, get a wife of your own to slap?"

'I would have said more, but my husband hit me—right across my mouth; and my mother-in-law hit me with the rolling pin. I thought they were going to kill me. Somehow, I managed to run out of the house and kept running in the darkness till I reached the park and hid behind a bush… I'm so unhappy… I want Rupa…'

~

Shri Tripathi let her cry for a few minutes. In any case, he needed time to think…

'I want my baby,' she repeated before he could decide what to say. 'I want Rupa. She must be so frightened.'

'Y-es…'

'And I don't want people to say nasty things about her. Ever.'

'I…'

'And I don't want them to beat me. It is against the law to beat women, I'm sure. It *is*, in our country.'

'Y-es.'

'And I don't want my husband to…touch me,' she said. 'Moreover, I'm going to have another baby. I didn't want it. I want it now. I don't want it to be harmed in any way.'

'When is, er…?'

'In November.'

That meant that she was four months pregnant, perhaps more. Shri Tripathi hoped the baby was not already harmed. He said a silent prayer. Then he telephoned the husband, introduced himself, told him that his wife was at his place and invited him over for a cup of tea and a talk.

'What is she doing at your place?' the husband cried, cutting him short. 'What is the bitch doing at your place? Where was she the whole night? Ask her to come home right away. Right away. Let me speak to her.'

She shook her head violently.

Shri Tripathi introduced himself to the husband once again, more slowly this time, followed that up with a few soothing sentences, and invited him once again to his house. There was no problem in the world, he added, that could not be sorted out over a cup of tea.

'I'm going to give her a hiding she will never forget,' the husband cried. 'Yes, I'm going to solve that problem once and for all.' But he turned up at Shri Tripathi's place in fifteen minutes.

'Where is Rupa?' Meera jumped up as he entered through the door.

'In the car outside,' the husband snapped, 'with ma.'

'Oh, has your mother come too?' Shri Tripathi said. 'Please ask her to join us.'

That was a mistake, for even as Shri Tripathi began to say, 'Marriage is like a stringed bow…' the woman took over.

'It may be so with you padhe-likhe people,' she said, dismissing all the educated people of the world with a wave of her right hand.

'Marriages don't work that way among us. For a marriage to work well, the wife has to know her place… In the olden days, wives used to know their place. Things changed after Indira Gandhi came to power. I was young then but I remember how she started spoiling women… Educated women are the worst. Look at this one,' she glared at Meera. 'She leaves the house in the middle of the night to go to God knows whom, leaving her child behind…'

'Er…' Shri Tripathi searched for something to stem the tide.

'It is not good for Rupa to hear all this,' he said. 'Such things leave scars.'

'And leaving your own child for the whole night does not leave scars? Humph!'

'It was due to, er…what happened last evening that she left home last evening,' Shri Tripathi said.

'So what if her husband beats her a bit?' the woman said. 'Is that cause to leave home? And it is for her own good that he beats her. Do you think my husband never beat me? What I can't understand is, how could she leave her child alone like this?'

Shri Tripathi tried to make peace, 'The child was not alone. It was with her father and—'

'God knows who her father is.'

Shri Tripathi's jaw dropped.

Meera exploded, 'What! What did you say? That Rupa is not my husband's child? Look at her eyes, her nose, her mouth, the shape of her head, the colour of her skin... Even a blind person will not say that she is not my husband's child.'

'I'm only saying what the whole world would say,' the mother-in-law muttered.

'Ma!' the husband found his voice. 'Leave that.' He rose. 'Let us go home,' he said, addressing Meera.

Meera gave Shri Tripathi a frightened glance.

'Er... That's quite right,' Shri Tripathi said. 'A wife's place is by the side of her husband. The important thing is for both sides to adjust. And as part of the adjustment, let us have no more beatings. Apart from everything else, it is illegal in this country to beat a woman. You can be sent to jail for that,' he gave the mother-in-law a pointed glance. She flinched. He continued, 'And if anything happens to an unborn child in this country,' he shook his head slowly before adding, 'only God can help you. So no beating. Is that understood?'

Nobody said anything.

'No doing anything that can hurt the unborn child,' he repeated, staring at the husband now. 'The Libyan law is quite clear on that point—and extremely severe. It can even...'

'I hope it is a son this time,' the mother-in-law interjected.

'Eh?' Shri Tripathi stopped.

'Women behave better when they have sons,' the woman added, as if by way of explanation.

Shri Tripathi took a deep sigh and counted till ten before continuing, 'Somebody from the Consulate will visit your place every month to see that all is well…' He waited.

Nobody said anything.

'I will pray for you,' he said, rising.

~

She visited him in office a couple of months later. She looked fuller than before, and thinner, he thought.

'I was passing this way—I'm going to hospital for a check-up—and thought of dropping in. How are you, sir?'

'How are *you*, beti?' he asked.

'In one piece,' she smiled.

'Hmm,' he gave her a dubious look. 'You don't look all that good.'

'This is the best I can look,' she said, 'suspended as I am between hell and God knows what will happen after the baby comes… My mother-in-law is holding a puja next Sunday so that all our friends and well-wishers can come to our place and pray that I get a son this time. Would you like to come?'

'I won't be in town that weekend—I've to go to Tobruk—but I'll also pray that you get a son,' Shri Tripathi said.

She rose.

A thought occurred to him. 'Have you written to your parents lately?'

'I had written to my younger sister, just a general letter, not mentioning anything. She wrote back that my father has stopped going out of the house and mixing in society—

thanks to me. And yes, he still does not want to see my face. Ever.'

~

A month passed. Then a month more. Shri Tripathi thought of her occasionally, mostly whenever his PA returned from a visit to her place and reported to him that all was well. But it was a busy time for him, full of tours, conferences, VIP visits...apart from the usual consular work.

One day, when he had just finished with a visitor to his office, the door of his office opened again and she walked in, with a baby in a sort of hamper strung in front of her, a backpack behind and a toddler by her side.

'How are you, beti?' he greeted her warmly and invited her to sit down.

She was leaving Benghazi, she said, sitting down carefully in a chair. The baby in the hamper was a girl, she said, her second daughter, now ten days old. The toddler was Rupa. 'Do namaste to dadaji,' she asked her. Rupa did a namaste.

He offered her tea. She said she had no time. Her plane was leaving in two hours.

'I've come to say goodbye,' she said, 'and to thank you for all your help... But I'm glad,' she added suddenly, 'that God did not listen to your prayer that I get a son. Otherwise, I might never have left...this hell.'

'But what will you do, beti?' he asked, feeling suddenly agitated. 'I could speak to your husband...'

'It is not his decision that I go,' she said. 'It is mine.'

'Oh! But where will you go? To Bulandshahr? I could write to your father if...'

'Thank you, sir. But no, I'm not going to Bulandshahr. I can't shame my father any further.'

'But...but...then where will you go?' he cried.

'India is a large country, sir, with many towns and many schools. There must be a school somewhere there that will have use for a maths teacher.' She stood up, adjusted the straps that held up her backpack, then the ones that held up her baby, took Rupa by the hand and walked out of his office.

Nora's First Love

We Marathas are great fighters. Not my cousin Atul Chitnis though. He is as gentle as a lamb. His Irish wife Isolde, whom he met when he was a medical student in University College, Dublin, and married soon after he joined Mater Hospital as an intern, is gentler, if anything. So are their sons Sean and Liam. Their daughter Nora, the youngest in the family, makes up for the lot.

~

'I was born a boy, you know,' she said to me solemnly the first time we met. She was a little over three years old at the time. 'I became a girl afterwards.'

'And a very pretty girl too!' I said. (I too had a daughter almost the same age back in Bombay and therefore knew what little girls liked to hear.)

'Hmm,' she looked at me suspiciously, as if being called pretty somehow detracted from the importance of having been born a boy. 'I have green eyes,' she said in the end. 'Green is the colour of Ireland,' she added defiantly.

~

She was probably eight when I visited Dublin the next time, again between business engagements in London. I recall I took her and her brother Liam to the Dublin zoo that Sunday. The zoo had just acquired a panda and Liam was keen to see it.

'Actually, my favourite animal is Raja, the elephant,' she said, after giving the panda a contemptuous glance and looking away, 'but he is ill in hospital.'

'What is wrong with him?' I asked.

'Actually, he has cirrhosis of the liver,' she said.

I didn't know that elephants could get cirrhosis but I was not going to show my ignorance to an eight-year-old. So I asked, 'How did he catch it?'

'Actually, he caught it when he was in the London zoo. When the English learnt that he had caught it, they quickly sold him to us... Never trust the English.'

'Er...but how did he catch it? Do you know?'

'He caught it from old vegetables and things that the English used to feed him. The English are the biggest penny-pinchers in the world.'

'Silly!' Liam cried irritably. 'You don't catch cirrhosis from vegetables. You catch it from drinking too much Guinness.'

'Who told you?' she cried hotly. 'David?'

'Er...' Liam looked away.

'David is a liar!' she said, addressing me. 'He is a Protestant, you see... Never trust a Protestant.'

~

The next time we met was in Bombay, when Atul brought the whole family to India to meet his relatives—and while at it, to do a bit of sightseeing. She was twelve years old at the time but she wore her hair short, and was so slim that she could pass for a boy. I took them round in my SUV, showing them the sights. She approved of us having renamed Victoria Terminus, the city's grand Indo-Saracenic railway station, *Chhatrapati Shivaji Maharaj Terminus*. She also approved of us having got rid of the name Bombay, which the English had given the city, and named it *Mumbai*. And she approved of us having removed all the British statues from the city's streets. She frowned when I said that the statues had been stored in a corner of a public garden. 'Throw them in the sea,' she advised. 'That's what I would do.'

'Easy, Nora!' I laughed. 'We Indians are non-violent people. And remember, you are fifty per cent Indian.'

She gave her father a quick glance; he smiled at her affectionately. She smiled back at him, squeezed his hand but turned to me again and said. 'You are right, but I would still throw those statues in the sea.'

~

A few more years passed. I was busy with my expanding business, now requiring me to visit Singapore and Dubai also, and had little time that I could call my own. But Atul was special. So when I got an invitation from him—really from Isolde—to attend their silver wedding party, I found some business to do in London and hopped across the Irish Sea to spend a few days in Dublin. Nora was nineteen now—and an absolute stunner, with an Ava Gardner face, a figure to match, and a peaches and cream complexion that even Ava Gardner would have killed for. On top of that, she still had those green eyes; and her hair, which she wore shoulder-length, had acquired a most startling tinge of flaming red. It was difficult to take one's eyes off her.

She was studying Irish history at the university, which, for all practical purposes, was the history of Irish resistance against British rule since time began. She was so immersed in it that she almost choked when she spoke of the potato famines that rapacious English policies had caused in Ireland in the nineteenth century. As for the 1916 Easter Rising in Dublin, she spoke of it as though it had happened yesterday. And tears came to her eyes when she spoke of Bobby Sands and the other hunger-strikers whom an uncaring world had allowed to starve to death in a Belfast prison. What galled her in particular was that just a few years after those deaths, the Irish Government had 'reached a deal' with the English that let the English hang on to Northern Ireland till the day the majority of its people asked for a change—which would never happen, she said, because the majority were Protestants. 'Moreover, the deal specifically rules out the use of violence!' she cried, her voice raised in outrage…

My last evening in Dublin she took me to a nightclub popular with IRA sympathizers in a lane off Grafton Street. We spent the evening drinking Guinness and singing rebel songs: 'Come out, ye Black and Tans, come out and fight me like a man…'; 'In 19 hundred and 16, the forces of the Crown / …ran from the rifles of the IRA'.

'Frankly, I am worried about Nora,' Isolde said to me when she drove me to the airport the next day. 'She talks of nothing the whole day except Catholics and Protestants, the English and the Irish, Sinn Fein and the Nationalists, Gerry Adams and Ian Paisley…and always, always, the IRA. All her friends are also like her. Crazy… Don't you think?'

'What does Atul say?' I asked. (What else could I have said?)

'Atul is so unworldly. He only laughs and says, "Relax, Isolde."'

~

As it should happen, I had to visit London on urgent business again some eight or nine months later, and telephoned Atul from London to say hello. Isolde picked up the phone.

'I'm so glad to hear your voice,' she said.

'And I'm glad to hear yours,' I said gallantly. 'How are you, Isolde?'

'No, I mean it,' she said. 'Could you come to Dublin?' she asked. 'Please…'

'Why? What has happened?' I asked, feeling suddenly worried for Nora.

'I… It is about Nora,' she stammered.

'What about her?'

'I can't tell you on the phone. But it is terribly important that you talk to her and stop her from… Oh, come for just a day if you are very busy. She listens to you; she has stopped listening to any of us.'

So I rescheduled a business meeting and caught the next Aer Lingus flight to Dublin, trying to guess the whole way what Nora could have done or, what seemed more likely from what Isolde had said, was planning to do. Could she have joined the IRA? Was she planning to participate in some terrible heroic action against the English?

I recalled how wistfully she had spoken of the IRA's bombing of a hotel in Brighton once that had almost succeeded in wiping out the entire British Cabinet, including the then Prime Minister, Margaret Thatcher.

Isolde was waiting for me in her car outside the airport. 'Nora wants to marry a boy from Saudi Arabia,' she told me the moment I got into the car and even before she had turned on the engine.

'What!'

'Yes,' she turned on the engine. 'Someone called Rashid-bin-something-or-the-other,' she slid the car out of the parking slot and took the exit for the highway.

'Where on earth did she meet him?'

'At a party some six or seven months back. He is also studying at DU. Business Administration. He told her he was new in Dublin and did not know anybody. She chatted with him the whole evening—she has always been nutty about underdogs—and before they parted, asked him to wave out to her the next time he saw her on the campus. He said it would be better if *she* waved out to him. Surprised, she asked him why he wouldn't wave out to her. He said because he might make a mistake and wave out to a wrong girl. "All Irish girls look alike to me," he said.'

'Oh!'

'Idiot!' Isolde cried. 'As if we Irish are blacks or something.' I kept quiet.

Isolde continued, 'As it happened, she saw him the very

next morning, waved out to him and they skipped a class to sip coffee in the college canteen—where he asked her some utterly stupid questions on Ireland, like *Is De Valera a common Irish name?* And *How can you make out who is a Protestant and who is not?* And *Why do even priests in Ireland drink alcohol?* Nora laughed and laughed and decided that he was the most charming fellow she had ever met—as well as a gentleman. He wouldn't let her pay for her share of the coffee, and had a brand new Lexus car, and insisted on opening the door of the car for her when he gave her a lift.

'Soon they began to meet every day,' Isolde continued. 'Then one day she invited him to the house for dinner. Remembering that Arabs don't eat pork, I had not made pork chops that evening. I had made stew. He asked me if the beef in the stew was halal. I said I had no idea. He said "Hmm" and then, "It doesn't matter. I'm not hungry anyway." I say, what sort of people are the Arabs?'

'Pretty much like other people,' I said, 'some good, some bad and some ugly.'

'Which category do the Saudi ones belong to?' she persisted.

'I, er…haven't had any special dealings with Saudis,' I said.

'Which means bad, I guess,' she said gloomily, 'or ugly.'

I laughed and protested that that was not what I had said.

'Anyway, this one is,' she continued. 'He already has a wife. Alive.'

'What!'

'Yes, in Saudi Arabia. Some place called Riyadh. Nora will be his second wife.'

'Good God! Does she know?'

'She is the one who told us.'

'And she still wants to marry him?'

'Yes. What is more, she is going to that place, Riyadh, to live with the first wife for a year, learn the language and get to know the customs of the country while the idiot finishes his studies at DU, and marry him thereafter. She has already applied for a job of English teacher in some school there and they have accepted her. She leaves next week. We have tried everything we can to stop her from committing this...suicide. She has stopped talking to us. You are our only hope. Please, please talk to her. Tell her that what she is planning to do is...just awful.'

~

I talked with her—for two whole hours. I pointed out to her the dangers strewn like mines along the path she was planning to take, about the pain she would cause her family, about the near certainty that the marriage would not work.

The result of all my talk? Zero. 'I love him,' is all she said in return.

'What about his first wife?' I asked.

'I will love her too,' she said, 'like a sister. And she will love me.'

'What if he marries yet again?' I persisted. 'These fellows can have up to four wives at a time, you know?'

'Rashid will never do that,' she said. 'He loves me.'

I changed tack.

'You will have to wear a hijab,' I said.

'What has that got to do with love?' she shot back.

I changed tack again.

'There are thousands of young Irishmen in Dublin alone,' I pointed out. 'Why marry an outsider?'

'There were thousands of young Irishmen in Dublin even when my mother got married,' she retorted. 'Why did she marry an outsider?... I'll tell you why. She married him because of love.'

I looked for a straw to clutch.

'What about Northern Ireland?' I asked, keeping a straight face. 'Are you going to abandon it to its fate? I thought you were going to fight to free it from the English.'

That got her. But she did not say anything, just stared at a window for a long time, her eyes brimming with tears. Then she wiped them with the back of her hand, got up and walked out of the room.

I returned to India, defeated. She flew to Riyadh a week later, determined to be worthy of the man she loved.

~

The first thing that did not run according to her script after that was the first wife's response to her wish to love her like a sister. She already had plenty of sisters, she told Nora. 'Moreover, you don't look like a sister at all... You look like an enemy,' she added. The wife had spoken in Arabic, so Nora had not understood a word of what she had said. But women have a way of conveying their feelings in such matters without the intermediary of a language. At least the first wife had. To cut a long story short, Nora moved out of the house the next morning and checked into a block of apartments favoured by expats working in Riyadh…

…only to get her next shock. People in Riyadh spoke Arabic, not English, and the little Arabic that she had picked up while sipping coffee with Rashid was hopelessly inadequate to the task of getting herself understood.

Then there was the problem of everybody staring at her—even though she had taken care to cover her head with a hijab. After three days of being stared at, she only wished she could turn invisible. The way to fulfil that wish came upon her suddenly that night, while watching a Saudi TV programme on correct clothing for women. The next morning, she bought herself a black abaya that covered her from top to toe. The staring stopped—only to be replaced by another problem. The abaya made her indistinguishable from Arab women, and therefore unqualified to go anywhere without a male escort. And she simply had to go to school and, occasionally, to shops.

Succour came in the form of a young doctor called Prem Lall, who lived in the same block of apartments. He took her shopping. The next day he drove her to school, assuring her that it was on the way to his hospital (his first lie), and, after she had poured her heart out to him that evening—the IRA, Rashid and all—telling her that he was from India (his second lie). In truth, it was his father who was from India. His mother was Irish (from Northern Ireland). Some thirty years back, when his mother was on a sightseeing trip to India with some friends, the two had met one Sunday in All Souls (Protestant) Church in New

Delhi, fallen in love and got married. Shortly after that, they had moved to Derry (her hometown) in Northern Ireland.

Prem did not tell any of this to Nora that evening. In fact, it was almost six months later, after they had spent hundreds of hours with each other, commuting, shopping, cooking, eating dinners together, etcetera, etcetera, that he told her about his father, mother and Derry…

There is not much more to tell of the story. They—Nora and Prem—returned to Ireland the next May, had a June wedding—in fact, three June weddings, the first in an accommodating Catholic church, the second in an accommodating Protestant church, and the last in a Hindu temple—and, soon thereafter, moved to Derry.

~

Time passed. I got news of Nora and Prem from Isolde from time to time. A year after they had got married, they had a baby, a girl, with green eyes and auburn hair promising to turn red. Two years later they had their second baby. Then a third… By the time Prem became Resident at the Derry General, they had become proud parents of five children. By the time he became Head of the Cardiac Unit of the hospital, they had added three more to the family.

~

I had spoken to Nora every time I visited Dublin in those years but had never gone north. I did so last month.

Nora still looked beautiful (or maybe I have entered the age when every woman looks beautiful) and I had a wonderful time chatting with her and a few of her eight children ('Not enough for a cricket team yet,' I joked to Prem when he returned from work). It was heartwarming to see him and Nora together…

Before leaving, however, I could not help teasing her. 'Whatever happened to the old Nora,' I asked, 'the one who so fervently wanted to free Northern Ireland from the English?'

'You forget, uncle,' she smiled. 'The future of Northern Ireland is going to be decided by the majority of its people… And all my children are Catholic!'

Madam Wants…

We had not invited Madam to India—she had invited herself—but we were delighted to have her. Her husband was the leader of a country awash in crude oil. If she went back happy, maybe he would sell us oil at a discount. From what we had heard, he had done that for one or two countries. He was a whimsical fellow.

However, we had no idea why she wanted to visit India, that too for just a day. She had not asked for a meeting with any minister, and she was accompanied by no more people than a maid and a security guard. So obviously her reason for coming to India was personal, not political. But what was it?

Did she wish to do some shopping? Arab women were crazy about Indian fabrics and jewellery…

Did she want to see a new Indian film? Arabs were crazy about our films too. And two Bollywood blockbusters were going to be released that week.

Did she want to go to a kathak dance? A qawwali mehfil? A ghazal session?… Three places in Delhi were staging special cultural events that week.

Did she want to visit Nizamuddin Auliya Dargah? Jama Masjid? The Qutb? Taj Mahal in Agra? Ajmer Sharif?…

Did she want to taste any of Delhi's famous kebabs, tandooris, biryanis, haleems, rumali rotis, pista kulfis, shahi tukdas?...

Did she want to see rain falling? (It was the rainy season in Delhi.) Many Arabs visited India just to see the rain. One Arab sheikh had been so thrilled to see it that he had stood by the open window of his hotel for hours, letting the water drench him—and ruin the curtains, carpets, everything...

Did she need to consult a doctor? I hoped not. She was only thirty-three and from what I had heard—I had never met her in person—a very fine woman, beautiful, refined, devoted to good deeds, a lady. It would be a pity if she had a health problem.

~

It fell on me to find out what she wanted—and to make sure that she got it. I was just a junior interpreter for Arabic in the Ministry in those days, and male to boot, but I was the only interpreter available at the short notice that she had given us. (She knew no English, in fact no language but Arabic.) So it was I who accompanied the Minister to the airport to receive her and to escort her to Rashtrapati Bhawan, where a VIP suite had been readied for her. The Minister left soon after we reached the place, giving me a meaningful glance that conveyed, 'Take care of her. It may save us a lot of money.' So it was again I who kept her company through the high tea, making small talk and wondering how I should ask her what she wanted.

Suddenly Madam put down her cup and said, 'I want to meet an astrologer.'

My mouth dropped. Just a year back, my wife and I had consulted Delhi's most famous astrologer, Pandit Pandey, to know if our next baby would be a boy. (We had three children already, all daughters.) The man had studied our palms and told us that our next baby would make us very happy and proud. Relieved, I had assured my mother, when my wife got pregnant a few weeks later, that she was going to deliver a boy this time… It had turned out to be a girl. I had sworn never to consult an astrologer again, and certainly not Pandit Pandey, a fraud if ever there was one.

'His name,' Madam continued, 'is Pandit Pandey.'

Naturally my mouth dropped again. I closed it quickly and tried to think of ways to change her mind. There was none. I sighed and brought out my mobile.

'Please do not tell him who I am,' Madam interrupted me. 'Tell him only that I am, er…a family friend, and that my husband is, er…a businessman in Dubai.'

'Very well, Madam,' I murmured, made a couple of calls and arranged for her to meet Pandit Pandey the first thing next morning.

~

'Tell him I have only one question to ask him,' she said as we entered the astrologer's lair, a dismal-looking kothi in Bengali Market.

'Yes, Madam,' I murmured and repeated her words to the astrologer, in Hindi.

The astrologer studied her hand for a few minutes and looked up. 'What is your question, Madam?'

'I want to know,' she said, 'whether my son will follow his father…?'

'You have two sons, Madam...' the astrologer paused. Madam gave me a quick glance. I shook my head violently, pleading innocence.

'I presume you are talking about your elder son,' the astrologer continued, not noticing (or feigning not to have noticed) our silent exchange.

'Na'am,' she nodded.

'May I see your hand again, Madam?'

He stared at the hand for a long time, then at something far away, then said in a murmur, 'He *will* follow his father...I fear.'

'Fear?' I blurted, in Hindi. He nodded gravely.

'How can I say that to her, Panditji? Her husband is an important man.'

'I know,' he said, just that.

I decided not to translate the last two words. 'He says your son *will* follow his father,' I said to Madam.

Madam's brows had gathered in a frown at the talk between Pandit Pandey and me. 'What else did he say?' she asked.

'Nothing else, Madam.'

'Hmm.' She stared at me for a long minute. I kept a straight face. She turned to Pandit Pandey, murmured a shokran, and asked me to hand over to him a bundle of hundred dollar notes she had given me to carry. I placed the bundle on the table between us.

'My fees,' Pandit Pandey said, 'are a hundred rupees per question, no more, no less.'

I translated.

Madam gave him a long look, as if trying to divine his thoughts. He stayed inscrutable. Finally, Madam asked me to substitute the bundle with a hundred-rupee note. I fished out a note from my wallet, placed it on the table, picked up the bundle of dollars, and followed her out of the room.

I gave her back the bundle in the car. She was silent all the way to Rashtrapati Bhawan. Her bags were packed and ready. The Minister was already there to escort her to the airport. They made polite talk in the car. I translated. 'Please don't tell anybody about my talk with the astrologer,' she said to me before boarding the plane.

On the way back the Minister asked me why she wanted to meet the astrologer.

'She wanted to know,' I lied, 'if her husband is planning to have a second wife.'

'Women!' he shook his head. 'They are the same everywhere, aren't they?'

~

Years passed. India got some oil from her country at a discount that year (and from time to time in the years that followed) but Madam did not visit Delhi again. Her husband did, to participate in a meeting of world's leaders on climate change. I had become a senior interpreter by then, but had a hard time translating his speech, so filled was it with virulent criticism of the West and its leaders—some of whom were present in the audience! I had to keep scrambling for softer substitutes for the words he used. Oil wealth, I said to my wife that day, had made him reckless, his own worst enemy. There was already no shortage of people who hated him: western leaders; directors of oil companies; Israelis; fellow Arab leaders; some of his own countrymen. They bowed almost 90 degrees when he gave them an audience, and sang his praise publicly when he gave them a contract or two, but in private they called him a fool, a mad man, a megalomaniac, a tyrant...

Two years later they brought him down. Nobody is sure how the rebellion began, who gave the rebels arms, who led them... But when the mob attacked the palace, there were no guards at the gates to stop them. The rebels stormed into the palace and made for the wide stairs to the upper floor. Bravely, he came out of his room to harangue them from the top of the stairs. They shot him, raced up the stairs, shot him again, then kicked and kicked and kicked him even though he was quite dead, then, remembering that there were more people in the palace to kill, spread out to look for them. They reached the back garden just when Madam and her sons, accompanied by a captain and a few soldiers, were fleeing from it. A shot brought down a soldier, another shot hit Anwar, the elder son. Madam screamed and turned back to hug the falling, dying boy. The captain wrenched her free of the boy and pushed her into a waiting Mercedes, then the dying boy, then himself in the front seat, even as more shots rang out, one of them hitting a second soldier, another hitting the rear fender. The next instant the car sprang forward, with only the captain in it to protect Madam and her sons across two hundred miles of a desert road...all the way to the border of the neighbouring country and then to the nearest hospital. Anwar was declared dead on arrival at the hospital.

~

Years passed. I was posted in the Indian High Commission in London now. Shreya, our youngest daughter, had just hit the headlines of all the newspapers in England—and the world—by swimming across the English Channel in record time. Everybody was calling to congratulate her—and us, the parents. Among the callers was the rector of a college in Oxford she had applied for admission to, offering her a scholarship.

When at last the telephone fell silent, and we were sitting down to lunch, it rang again. 'I'll take it,' I said, getting up from the table.

'Kayfa halak?' the voice said softly.

Eighteen years had passed since I had heard the voice last, at the airport in Delhi, but I recognized it instantly.

'I am well, Madam. How are you?' I asked.

'I am well too, Allah shokran. I have called to congratulate you for your daughter's great achievement.'

'Thank you, Madam. I will tell her.'

'Daughters are truly Allah's gifts to mankind.'

'Thank you.'

A moment of silence passed.

'I live in Lausanne now,' she said.

I knew that. 'How is Abbas?' I asked, suddenly remembering the name of her second son.

'He is married now. They live in Zurich.'

I fell silent again. There was something in her voice that suggested the son had grown distant from her.

'I want to ask you something,' she said after another moment.

'What, Madam?'

'Exactly what did the astrologer say that day in Delhi?'

I hesitated, but told her. A minute more passed. I could hear her breathing. Then another minute. I could not hear the breathing any more. 'Madam?' I cried. 'Madam?'

She let out a sigh. 'He was a sweet and gentle boy. He should not have died... *I* should have.'

Only an Indian Wife

Sridhar is an income tax officer. He is also an old friend of mine and, for many years now, my partner in the annual tennis tournament of our club, the Delhi Gymkhana. We play well together though, till last year, we had never been able to cross the crucial semifinal hurdle. Last year we crossed it, and crossed it dramatically, knocking out the top-seeded pair in two straight sets, 6-4, 6-3. Many newspapers the next morning said, and we too felt, that we had a real chance to win the final on Sunday and thereby to create history. Never before had any pair with both the players on the wrong side of forty won the men's doubles.

On late Friday night, however, Sridhar got a telephone call from his Chairman, asking him to meet him at his home first thing the next morning.

~

'Do you know a Joint Commissioner called Hiralal Motilal Jain?' he asked him after a servant had served them tea and left. 'He works in our office in Connaught Place.'

Sridhar said no, he did not know him.

'His name is in the list of officers to be considered for promotion next week,' the Chairman said. 'Before I send the list to the Board, I want to make sure that the fellow is all right. I've a hunch that he is not.'

'A hunch, sir?'

'Yes,' the Chairman said, 'that too because of something that happened almost thirty years ago. I was a Deputy Commissioner in Delhi in those days and he a clerk in our office—one of the many dozens. He came to our notice only because he placed an advertisement for a bride in the *Hindustan Times*, mentioning that he was an income tax official and inviting interested parties to write to him, quoting the amount of dowry they were prepared to pay…

'Naturally, the advertisement created a stir in the Department and an enquiry was ordered. Nothing came of it. Taking dowry, though illegal, was still the done thing in those days—so long as it was done discretely. Moreover, in Jain's case, there were no witnesses and no aggrieved parties, let alone any FIR filed with the police. Just the advertisement. And the fellow himself kept saying that he had nothing to do with it; some unnamed enemy of his must have placed the ad… In the end, we had to close the enquiry. But the name—Hiralal Motilal Jain—stayed in my mind, probably because soon after that he married the daughter of a shady lawyer in Tees Hazari court, the type that milks his clients, collects his fees in cash, and rarely, if ever, pays his taxes. I had no doubt in my mind that Jain had got his dowry.

'A month or two later, I was transferred to Cochin. Years passed. Our paths never crossed again—till yesterday, when I got a call from, er…somebody in the PMO, saying that Jain was a fine officer, fully deserving the promotion, and I remembered the dowry affair. It also occurred to me that the climb from clerk to Joint Commissioner, even in thirty years, was too much of a good thing. So was also, of course, the call from the PMO. Clearly, something about the man was not right. And I decided that we should do a background check on him before forwarding his name to the Promotion Board. And I thought of you, remembering the way you handled the Goa case… Can you do the check, Sridhar? Can you find out if Jain takes bribes? Can you at least find out if he has assets disproportionate to his known sources of income?'

'How soon do you want to know that, sir?' Sridhar asked.

'I'm afraid the Board is meeting on Monday,' the Chairman said.

Sridhar hesitated. It was already Saturday morning. He would have just about forty-eight hours to find out if a Joint Commissioner in the Income Tax Department was corrupt. Moreover, on Sunday afternoon he was to play the most important tennis match of his life, the Gymkhana Final. If he did not win the men's doubles cup this time, he would never win it. At the same time, the Chairman was a decent man, struggling against heavy odds to clean up the system…

'I'll try, sir,' he said to the Chairman.

'Thank you,' the Chairman rose. 'You will, of course, exercise the utmost care while making your investigation. Nobody should get wind of it. Indeed, that is why—to preserve secrecy—I suggested that we meet here and not in my office. The offices of Delhi leak like a sieve.'

~

We lost the final (6-0, 6-1) and we lost it in thirty-six minutes flat, which, I suppose, has made history of sorts. To us, however, it was a nightmare. The spectators did not even boo us when the match ended. They just watched us with pitying eyes as we picked up our kits and, with our heads hanging low, made our way out of the court, into the Men's changing room, and by and by, into a dark corner of the bar.

'I'm sorry,' Sridhar murmured after I ordered the beers. 'I wasn't myself today.'

'Forget it,' I said, though I knew that it was going to take a long time for either of us to forget his play, double-faulting his serves, fluffing his smashes, lobbing lollypops to the opponents…

Neither of us said anything more till the beers came. Then I picked up my glass and said 'Cheers!'

He too picked up his glass, but only to put it down again and said, 'I owe you an explanation.'

'Explanation?'

'Why I was not myself today.'

And he told me about his meeting with his Chairman.

~

'But what happened after the meeting?' I asked. 'I mean, what did you discover about this Jain fellow that has upset you so much?'

He told me…

'After I left the Chairman's house, I weighed my options. Clearly I had no time to take the usual path: look up old records, talk to people who may have known Jain or may have dealt with him at his various postings, hack into his email correspondence, have him followed, etc. There was really only one thing to do—to bug his house, and hope against hope that he would betray himself in the few hours available to me.

'By noon I had a bugging device installed in his house. Installing those devices is always the easiest part. It was especially so in this case because Jain was away in office, and their morning maid had come and gone. There was nobody at home except Jain's wife to let in the "technician from the telephone department" to "check the wiring". That done, I sat in my office by the receiver that relayed sounds transmitted by the device and waited.

'A dreary afternoon passed, relieved only by Jain's wife talking to various women on the telephone about servants, clothes and, specially, other women, all members of some kitty group which seemed to have gone through a rough patch lately. In the evening, a maid came to the house to cook the evening meal, which provided more relief, for the woman was in a chatty mood and had some interesting things to say about goings-on in the household where she works in the mornings. But an hour later, she too left and silence returned. Jain came home late at night, and for a brief moment my hopes rose as the wife began to talk about Atul, their son, studying in New York, which costs money. But Jain said, "Look, I've had a hard day. I'm in no mood to listen to any stupid talk tonight," and there was no more talk about the son. In fact, the only sounds that I could hear after that were those of two people eating a sullen meal, then sitting before the TV for half an hour, switching channels, and at last, after brief visits to the bathroom, going to bed, probably with their backs turned to each other.

'I guess I too dozed off soon thereafter. I must have overslept, for it was already eight when I woke up, and the telephone in the Jain bedroom was ringing. It was from their daughter, who too is apparently studying in America and who had called to say that she had reached Honolulu safely—for a holiday. Not much meat there, except inferentially. I waited. Half an hour later, there was another call, this one from their son Atul, and some heated but confusing exchanges followed, with all three of them, father, mother and the boy talking at the same time. It was impossible to follow who was saying what. All that I could gather was that the boy wanted to marry somebody who was prepared to wear saris. Jain cut short the telephone with "I'll call you back", banged down the telephone and presumably stomped out of the room. At least my bugging receiver turned silent once more.

'Half an hour later, the receiver came to life again. Jain had returned from wherever he had stomped to, but to a waiting wife. In no time at all they were back to where they were before, exchanging views on Atul's marriage plans. Mercifully, there were only two of them talking this time, so I could get the gist of the problem.

'The girl that Atul wanted to marry was an American girl by the name of Laura, and Jain's wife was opposed to the very idea of having a foreign bahu. Only an Indian wife, she kept saying to her husband, can walk properly in a sari—till our man could take it no more. "Oh, hang your bloody sari," he cried. "Let the girl walk in a bikini if she wants. Do you know that her father is the CFO of Goldman Sachs? Do you have any idea what it means to be the only daughter—the only child—of the *Chief Financial Officer* of Goldman Sachs? She is an heiress! A dollar heiress!"

'That shut up the wife, but not for long. Soon she returned with fresh ammunition, that only an Indian wife can touch the feet of the elders with becoming grace, till Jain cried, "Oh, hang your feet. What does it matter how she touches people's feet, or if she touches them at all? Can't you get it through your thick skull that she is rolling in money?"

'One more minute of silence followed. Then the wife came up with yet another argument, that only an Indian wife can roll chapatis properly round. To which he said something that sounded like, "Ohhh, shove your chapatis. Order them from the Oberoi if you want to."

'And thus it went, till, exhausted from listening to arguments for and against marrying Laura, I was about to leave my room for a much-needed visit to the bathroom, when suddenly the wife exploded, "Money, money, money. That's all you can think of. There is money coming out of our ears: lakhs of rupees, crores of rupees... What do we need more money for?" At which Jain hastened to say, dropping his voice several notches, "Sh... Walls have ears." To which she replied, raising her voice several notches, "Yes. Like the wall in our bathroom. You can't even pee there without money staring at you."'

~

'Then?' I asked Sridhar, as he paused to take a big gulp of beer, as if to fortify himself for some ordeal, but emptying the glass in the process. I quickly ordered two more beers.

'Then we raided the place,' Sridhar said, 'I, my PA—he is an amateur photographer—and a cousin of mine who works in the CBI. We had to get proof. Taped conversation is not admissible evidence in a court of law.'

'And you found the money…'

He nodded. 'We didn't need the help of any Sherlock Holmes to find it. We knew exactly where to look for it.'

'How much?' I asked.

'Four crore and fifty-seven lakhs.'

I whistled.

'Yes,' Sridhar said. 'Four hundred and fifty bundles of 1,000-rupee notes and the loose change.'

'Then?' I asked.

'I asked Jain where he had got the money from.'

'What did he say?'

'"Money?" he said parrot-like, as if he had no idea what I was talking about.

'"Yes, money," I said, pointing my thumb to the bundles piled high on his dining table and now being photographed by my PA.

'He squinted at the piles as if had never seen them before and said he had no idea where they had come from. They were not his.

'"Then whose?" I asked.

'"Mine," his wife said suddenly. "The money is mine."

'I had not noticed her till then. I noticed her now: fifty-ish, short, solid, big-bosomed. A tuft of hair came out of a mole on her chin.

'"Very well, madam," I said, "then please tell us how you got it."

'"I got it from my customers," she said.

'"I see," I said. "Customers. And what, exactly, is your business, madam? Clothes? Jewellery? Beauty parlour?..."

'"None of those," she said. "I'm in the entertainment business."

'"I see," I said, thinking that she meant films or TV or music.

'"And where exactly is your place of work?" I asked.

'"Right here," she said.

'"Here?" I repeated, surprised. "Where here?" I looked round the room.

'"In the bedroom," she said.

'The camera dropped from my PA's hand. He gave me a very-sorry look and scrambled to pick it up. I looked at Jain. He was staring in an awestruck sort of way at his wife. I looked at her. She was staring back at him. Conspiratorially? Defiantly? I could not tell. I looked at my CBI cousin. He gulped and gave me a what-have-we-got-into sort of look.

'"I see," I said when I found my voice again, and added, as if seeking confirmation from her, "In the bedroom, is it?"

'"Yes," she said.

'"Do you know, madam," I asked, "that prostitution is a crime?"

'"It is not," she said. "Soliciting is a crime. And I don't solicit," she added. "The customers come to me on their own."

'"Aha," I said. "And how do they know that you are, er…in the entertainment business, madam?"

'"By word of mouth," she said.

'"Four crore and fifty-six lakh rupees is a lot of money," I said.

'"I've a lot of customers," she said.

'"Hmm. And who are these customers, madam?" I asked. "May I have their names please?"

'"That would be giving away trade secrets," she said. "You don't expect me to give away my trade secrets, do you?" She pursed her lips and folded her arms.

'I searched for something new to say and stumbled into asking, "And when did you have your last customer, madam?"

'"Oh…about an hour back," she said.

'"Your husband was at home at the time," I pounced.

'That fixed her, but only for a moment. "No, he wasn't," she said. "He had stepped into the verandah for a smoke. I don't like the smell of cigarette smoke in the house."

'"I suppose your customers too don't like the smell of cigarette smoke," I said sarcastically.

'"That's right," she cried, her eyes narrowed in anger.

'Clearly this line of questioning was taking me nowhere. I wondered what to say next and looked around for help. My CBI cousin was still under some sort of spell but my PA stepped close and whispered in my ear what seemed like a more promising line of questioning.

'"Madam," I said, turning to the wife again, "may I please see your income tax statements of the last five years?"

'"You can't," she said.

'"I can't?" I raised an eyebrow. "Why, may I ask?"

'"Because there are none," she said.

'"What! And why not, may I ask?"

'"Because I started the business only this year," she said.

'"I see," I said. "Then may I see the advance payment receipt for the last quarter, madam?"

'"There isn't any advance payment receipt either," she said. "I started the business only this quarter. My first advance payment is due on the 15th of December."

'"That's today!" My CBI cousin finally woke up to point out. Idiot!

'"That's right," she said. "So, if you people would please leave my house, I can still go to my bank and pay the advance tax—*and* deposit the money in my account. I don't want to keep so much money at home. Anybody can take it away," she added, covering all three of us in a slow, sweeping glance.

'I had reached the end, I knew. I took one last look at Jain, who was edging towards the piles on the table, my PA, making for the exit, my CBI cousin, already on the other side of it...and somehow made my way to the door. All that work for nothing. At the door, however, I turned to take a parting shot. "Your father, I believe, was a lawyer, madam. Was he, by any chance, a taxation lawyer?"

'"Yes, he was," she snapped. "He used to say that there are just two kinds of income tax officers, those who are corrupt and those who are not *yet* corrupt."

'We stared at each other across the room. Then, unable to contain myself, I cried, "I'm a hard-working man myself, madam, but I bow to you. You must be the hardest working person in the whole city."

'She did not say anything to that. She just stepped forward and banged shut the door. I returned to office.'

~

Sridhar emptied his glass and rose from his chair to go when he finished the story. 'Shall we?'

I tried to think of something soothing to say as I scrambled to finish my drink and get up. 'At least you had the last word,' I said. 'That's something.'

'No,' he said. 'She had the last word.'

'How?' I asked.

'The receiver in my office was still on when I returned there. As I made to switch it off, I heard her voice, loud and clear. I paused to listen.

'"And never forget, my dear husband," the voice said, "only an Indian wife can make such a sacrifice—ruin her whole reputation—for the sake of her husband."'

A Gifted Child

It was his first visit to his daughter after his parting from his wife. It had been a painful parting. It still hurt to think that she had cheated on him. Yes, theirs had been an arranged marriage. Yes, he was over thirty years old and she barely twenty when they got married. But he had been a good husband and father, he was sure. And theirs had been a happy, almost model marriage. Everybody had said so at their silver anniversary party.

He had learnt of her affair—with her yoga instructor, of all people—though an anonymous letter to his office address. 'Everybody in Delhi knows of it,' the hateful writer had added. He had gone home and confronted her with the letter. She had denied everything at first, but soon broken down—she never could lie—confessed all and promised not to see the man again. A week later, she had broken the promise. He had learnt of it through a second anonymous letter, this one accompanied by photographs, and he had walked out on her. He had not asked her for a divorce, not even for a legal separation. Those were of no use to him, he had decided after a few days of solitude in a hotel room. He was almost sixty years of age and had a number of health problems, not all of which could be dismissed as mere aches and pains of creeping old age. For one, he had half a lung missing; he also had a cardiac condition; and he had diabetes that invariably got worse under stress. He did not have many years to live. In any case, all that he wanted in life now was peace in his heart. He had tried to get it through work, through books, and, one terrible night, through whisky. The pain had never gone away.

Their daughter, telephoning both of them from California—she could not come to India because of her baby—had tried to bring them together again.

'How could you do something like this, ma?' she had admonished the mother. 'At your age too…'

'You won't understand,' the mother had murmured.

'Why can't you leave that horrid man?'

'He… You won't understand.'

'You don't know how much you have hurt papa.'

'I'm sorry for that. I didn't mean to hurt him. I tried to tell him that. He was not interested in talking about—'

'What is the point of saying sorry if you are not prepared to leave that man? Why can't you leave him?'

'I…can't.'

'Come to California, ma. Tara wants you. Ask nana-nani to come here, she says.'

'Give Tara a hug and a kiss from me. Tell her I will Skype her tomorrow night.'

'Come here, ma.'

'I…can't at the moment. Maybe later.'

~

'I miss you, papa,' she had said to her father. 'Tara also misses you.'

'I miss her too,' he had said. 'She is a joy to talk to. Whoever is teaching her to talk like this?'

'She is a gifted child… But talking with her on Skype is not the same thing as being with her. Come to us, papa.'

'I wish I could. But I have no more leave to my credit. I used up all of it when we came there for Tara's birthday. I'm afraid I can come there again only after I retire.'

'On the 31st of May next year?'

'That's right.'

'But May is so far…'

'Yes… Please give Tara a kiss and a hug from me.'

'I love you, papa.'

'I love you more.'

The pain had come back the instant he had said it. *I love you / I love you more* was what he used to say to *her*—and she to him.

~

Then, one day a few months later, she had caught the yoga instructor in bed with a new pupil. Hours and then days of bitter recriminations had followed, till one day she had woken up with the realization that she did not want him any longer. What she wanted was to win back the love and trust of the man she had wronged, her husband. She had telephoned him, told him everything, added that she truly repented what she had done and asked him, amid sobs, to return to her.

He had taken a long time before speaking, and then

mumbled, 'I'm sorry. You must... I'm very sorry. But no, I can't come back.'

'I love you,' she had cried.

'I'm sorry,' he had repeated.

Now she too wanted nothing more in life than peace in her heart. She had turned to God for that, and by and by become one of the many women that frequented the local Arya Samaj ashram every day. But the pain had refused to go away.

~

He left for California the day he retired, taking with him, among other gifts, a jigsaw puzzle of the Taj Mahal for Tara. She gave him a hug when he handed her the box and eagerly poured out the pieces from it. Alas, it turned out to be too difficult for her.

'But papa!' his daughter examined the box and cried. 'This puzzle is meant for children of six years of age. Tara is only two years and ten months old!'

He scratched his head and mumbled. 'I thought that since she is a gifted child...'

'Papa!' The daughter smiled and shook her head, conveying what she thought of his thinking.

He made up with Tara by taking her to a toyshop in a nearby mall the next day to buy her a jigsaw puzzle of her choice. She selected a soft toy, a dinosaur, instead. Then he took her on a ride in a toy train that meandered through the mall. Finally, he gave her a special treat—a slice of pizza (and an ice cream for himself)—sitting at a table by a pretty fountain in an outdoor cafe.

'It is a wish fountain,' he told her. 'You throw a coin in it and make a wish. See! There are coins in the fountain.' She leaned over the ledge of the fountain to see coins shimmering at the bottom of the fountain. 'Do you want to make a wish?' He gave her a coin to throw in the fountain. 'Make a wish.'

'What wish?' she asked, closing her fist round the coin.

'Any wish,' he said. 'Like for a dolly…'

'But I already have a dolly…'

'…or shoes that light up when you walk in them…'

'I already have shoes that light up…'

'Er…make any wish.'

She threw in the coin, leant forward and watched it sink.

'What wish did you make?' he asked.

'Oh! I forgot to make a wish,' she laughed. 'Give me another coin.'

He gave her another coin. She promptly threw it into the water and watched it sink.

'What wish did you make?' he asked again.

'Oh! I forgot again,' she laughed.

The pizza came, along with his ice cream. He held up the slice before her mouth for her to eat and, as she ate it, made a silent wish: May she laugh all her life; may she never know pain… The ice cream melted in the bowl.

'I saw a monster in my dream last night,' she said suddenly.

'Really?'

She nodded. 'Fire was coming out of its mouth. And its tail was swishing left and right.'

'Did it have a horn on its head, like a unicorn?'

'No, but it had lots of teeth.'

'Like a crocodile?'

'No, like an alligator. You know the difference between the two, don't you?'

'Er...yes. So what did you do?'

'I shut my eyes tight and the monster went away. When you shut your eyes tight, bad dreams go away,' Tara nodded her head again.

'That's right,' he said.

He drove back by the coastal route, first shifting the child's seat on the sea-side. She loved to see the waves, he knew.

'One day, when I was little,' she said, 'daddy took me into the waves. I saw a dolphin in the sea.'

'Really? Were you scared?'

'No... Dolphins don't bite.'

'I would have been scared,' he said.

'*I* will come with you,' she said. 'Then you will not be scared.'

'Yes. Then I will not be scared.'

When they reached home, he helped her out of the seat, carried her to the door and let her ring the bell, once, twice... His daughter opened it.

'See my Dino, mummy,' Tara held out the dinosaur for her to see.

'Did you thank nana for it?' she asked.

'I forgot... Thank you, nana.'

'You are a sweetheart,' he said, giving her a kiss.

'You should say "You are welcome" when people say "Thank you",' she said.

'You are welcome,' he said, gave her another kiss and passed her to her mother's waiting arms.

~

That night, before taking her to bed, the mother asked Tara to say good night to him.

'Good night, nana,' she said.

'How about giving me a hug?' he asked.

'But I gave you a hug today morning,' she said.

The mother intervened. 'Not *today* morning, Tara, say *this* morning.'

'*This* morning,' she said.

'That was a good-morning hug,' he said. 'You have not given me a good-night hug.'

She frowned, as if weighing what he had said. He waited.

'Okay,' she said after a few moments, and gave him a hug.

~

Thursday passed. Then Friday and Saturday. He spent the days babysitting: taking her to the children's park, the mall, the wishing fountain again, the neighbourhood grocery shop, the zoo...chatting with her, playing with her, feeding her...

He got up late on Sunday morning. Tara was already in her high chair in the dining room, eating a buttered toast and talking (he thought) with her mother. It was only when he bent over her to give her a kiss that he noticed the laptop lying open two feet from her and realized that she was talking to her grandmother, his wife, on Skype. He stepped out of the range of the laptop and looked at it… She had stopped dyeing her hair, he noticed. And her eyes had a sadness he had never seen before. He looked away and wiped the tears that had suddenly come to his eyes.

'I love you, darling,' he heard her say the next moment and started. But she was talking to Tara.

'Come to my house, nani,' Tara said. 'Number 3163, Plum Tree Drive.'

'I'll try and remember that.'

'But I will come to the airport and bring you. Otherwise you will get lost.'

'Thank you…'

'I will come with nana. He can drive the car.'

'Hmm.'

'Nana is scared of dolphins.'

'Hmm.'

~

Sunday evening. Tara was humming to herself and arranging her soft toys on a sofa: a teddy bear, a cheetah, a doll, a puppy, the dinosaur… Her mother, standing by a counter in the open kitchen, was preparing her milk bottle. Her father, slouching in an easy chair on her right, was surfing the world with his smart phone. He—her grandfather—was bent over a low table, struggling to set up the track of a toy train he had bought for her that afternoon.

'I've fixed the bridge of the train. See, Tara!' he pointed at the arched bridge for her to see.

She gave the bridge a brief glance, saw that the track

was not yet finished, and returned to her toys, rearranging them in a descending order, then in an ascending order, talking to them all the while.

Suddenly she stopped to look at the teddy bear, then turned and looked critically at her grandfather.

'Nana, you are fat,' she said.

'Am I?' He looked at his stomach and looked up. 'Are you sure?'

She pursed her lips and nodded her head.

'Maybe I am not sitting properly,' he said, sitting up straight and sucking in his stomach. 'Now do I look fat?'

She nodded.

'Is mummy fat?'

She shook her head.

'Is daddy fat?'

She shook her head.

'Is nani fat?' he heard himself asking. She shook her head.

'Only I am fat?'

She nodded. 'You and Teddy.'

He gave Teddy a glance. 'I suppose I *am* fat,' he said after a moment, making a sad face. 'But I don't want to be fat. I want to be slim, like you. What should I do to become slim?'

'You should do like this,' she said, jumping on the spot three times.

'I did that yesterday,' he said, 'but I'm still fat.'

'Then you should do like this,' she said, raising her arms sideways and going round on the spot twice.

'I did that too,' he said. 'I'm still fat.'

'Then you should do like this,' she said, bending forward till her head was resting on the carpet.

'Are you sure?' he asked.

'Yes,' she said from the carpet.

'Thank you for telling me.'

'You are welcome,' she said, standing up.

'I'll do it tomorrow,' he continued.

'You should do it today,' she said.

'Tomorrow morning?'

'No. Today...'

'That's enough, Tara,' her mother said sharply.

But the girl had not finished. 'You are lazy,' she said to him.

'I'm not lazy,' he said. 'I'm only...'

'You are. You are. You should stand in the corner there and not make any noise.'

'I said, that's enough, Tara,' her mother cried, hurrying close and seizing her by the arm. 'Say sorry to nana.'

'We are only playing,' he said.

'No, papa,' the mother said. 'You are spoiling her. Say sorry to nana,' she repeated to the girl.

'No!' she said.

'SAY SORRY!'

Tara bit her tongue, gave him a resentful glance and, turning away, mumbled, 'Sorry.'

'Hmm...' The mother studied her for a moment, as if wondering if that was enough.

The clock chimed.

'Oh,' the mother looked at the clock. 'Time for bed. Come on.'

'But it is not eight o'clock,' the girl said.

'It *is* eight o'clock,' said the mother. 'See the clock there? The small hand is pointing to eight. That means it is eight o'clock. Time for little girls to go to bed.'

'But you said I'm a big girl now,' the girl said. 'Remember? You said it when I fell down today morning—this morning… You blew on my knee and said I must not cry because I'm a big girl now.'

'All right, you are a big girl. But it is still time for you to go to bed.'

'But I'm talking with Dino.'

'You can talk with him in bed. Pick him up,' the mother said. 'Come on.'

'But my dolly feels lonely if I leave her.'

'She has Teddy for company, as well as the puppy and the cheetah.'

'But…'

'No more talk. Just pick up Dino.'

The girl sighed and picked up the dinosaur.

'Daddy will take you to bed and feed you milk,' the mother said.

The father put the phone in his pocket, rose from the easy chair and ruffled the girl's hair. 'Come on, big girl.'

'Now say good night to nana,' the mother reminded.

'No!'

'Tara!'

'Good night, nana,' the girl mumbled.

'How about giving me a good-night hug, Tara,' he said.

'No!' she said.

'Just a small hug,' he said.

'No!' she repeated.

The father's phone rang. 'It is from a client,' he checked it and said. 'I'll have to take it.'

'Hmm,' the mother hesitated. 'Nana will feed you milk,' she decided.

'No!' the girl said. '*You* feed me milk.'

'I have work to do,' the mother said. 'Nana will feed you milk.'

'I too have work to do,' he said quickly, giving the mother a wink. 'Tara will drink the milk by herself. She is a big girl now. Aren't you, Tara?'

Tara looked at him uncertainly.

'But I will carry the milk bottle to your room and switch on the light for you, Tara,' he added, taking the bottle from the mother's hand. 'You carry Dino, okay?' He offered her his finger.

She wavered for a moment but took the finger.

'Shall we show Dino the mirror in the bathroom?' he asked when they reached the bedroom. 'He has never seen a mirror.' Then, without waiting for her reply, he put the milk bottle on a side table, picked her up, Dino in hand, switched on the bathroom light and stepped into it. The bathroom had two washbasins. Hanging on the wall behind the basins were two large, identical, oval-shaped mirrors set in ornate gilt frames. He stood before the mirror on the left.

She looked at Dino in the mirror for a moment, then at herself. A few moments passed.

'Who is the pretty girl in the mirror?' he asked her. 'The one with the big, black, beautiful eyes...'

She did not say anything, just continued looking. When at last she opened her mouth, she said, 'Now the other mirror.'

He moved sideways till they were facing the other mirror.

'Who is the pretty girl in the mirror?' he asked again.

She replied this time. 'Tara,' she said.

'Y-es,' he said. 'She is the prettiest girl in the world. Who made her so pretty?'

'Mummy,' she said. 'Mummy and daddy.'

'Y-es.'

A few more moments passed.

'How about some milkoo now?' he asked.

She came out of the trance. 'I like cold milkoo,' she said.

'It *is* cold,' he said, carrying her to her bed. 'See!' She touched the bottle.

He stroked her hair as she drank the milk, her head held up by a couple of soft pillows, her baby blanket resting lightly on her, her right hand clutching the dinosaur. Her eyes turned sleepy before she had finished the milk. She finished it nevertheless and, as he took away the empty bottle, murmured, 'I love you, nana—also nani.' Then she rolled away from the pillows and fell fast asleep.

'I love you more,' he said. Then he rearranged the blanket on her, kissed her gently, got up and walked to the door. He stopped at the door and turned back for one last look at her. 'Yes,' he murmured again, 'I love you more.' He switched off the light, stepped out of the room, half closed the door behind him and looked at his watch. It was almost nine o'clock. Nine-thirty in the morning in Delhi. He went to his room, poured himself a glass of water and stood with it before the large window. A moon was rising over the roof of the house across. He watched it for a long time... Then he put down the glass, took out his mobile and proceeded to press the buttons. He did not have to look up the number. He knew it by heart.

One Memorable Day

For almost three years after they got married they were happy. He worked as a pharmacist in Mumbai Pharmaceuticals. She finished her MA (Sociology) and after that began to do fieldwork for her thesis on communal harmony. Twice a year they visited his parents in Nagpur and hers in Ratnagiri. The year she got her MA they even went to Goa on a glorious holiday… All that cost money. Yet almost every month they were able to save a part of his salary.

Then suddenly one day the company that he was working for closed down without warning. And the only job that he could find after months of search was that of a mixer of paints in a building company. It was not the sort of job that anyone with his qualifications should take, but their savings had dipped to a frightening figure over the months and he took the job 'for the present'. It broke her heart to see him accept the 'lowly' job. He could have waited for a better one, she realized, if she too had been working for money… She decided to take up a job.

To her shock, the only job that postgraduates in sociology were deemed fit for was teaching the subject to undergraduates. Unfortunately, there was no vacancy for that in any college in Mumbai. There was an opening in a college in Ratnagiri, but she would rather die than live away from him. In desperation she tried to get the job of a high school teacher, even a primary school teacher. Every school she approached told her that to become a teacher she needed a BEd degree. It did not matter that she had secured a first in MA, knew four languages well—English, Konkani, Marathi and Hindi—and could handle the computer with the speed of a teenager. And it did not matter that she had played hockey for her college. What she needed was that wretched BEd degree.

She tried to get a non-teaching job—in the government, in the media, in advertising... All to no avail. There seemed to be hundreds of applicants for every decent job in Mumbai.

~

Then one morning she lost her purse. She had taken an auto-rickshaw from Parel—they lived in a single room in an old tenement there—to Bombay Hospital for an interview for a job. The auto driver was good but the traffic was terrible. It came to a complete halt when the auto was still a couple of furlongs from the hospital. Anxious not to be late for the interview, she had brought out from her purse the exact amount she would need for the fare and was holding the notes in her hand. As minutes ticked by without the traffic moving an inch, she gave the money to the driver, jumped out of the auto and ran all the way to the hospital. She remembered the purse only when asked to show the letter from the hospital inviting her for the interview. She ran back to where she had left the auto, hoping against hope. But the traffic was flowing once more; the auto was nowhere in sight; her purse was gone.

She went to the nearby police station and told the first person in uniform she saw there, a portly man stepping out of a jeep, what had happened. She had never before done anything so foolish, she added. Could the police please help her find the purse? She simply could not afford to lose the papers and other things in it.

The man—he happened to be a superintendent of police—was sympathetic but not hopeful. Mumbai, he said, was no longer a particularly honest place, not like it was thirty-three years back, when he joined the police. It was all because of the millions of outsiders that had migrated to the city, he sighed. 'Anyway, file your report and we will see what we can do.' He invited her into his room, offered her a cup of tea and called in a havaldar to take down her report.

'What does the purse look like?' he guided her.

She described the purse. It was deep crimson in colour, made of artificial leather, and it closed with a clasp. It had a matching strap and a pocket on one side that closed with a zip.

'Where did you lose it?'

She described where—and how—she had lost it.

'Did you, by any chance, notice the number of the auto?' he asked.

The number was written on the fare meter, she said. Unfortunately, the paint had come off two of the digits. So the number she remembered (MH 03_ 7 _ 824) was not complete. It was an old auto, she added, with almost bald tires, a slightly bent front fender and two dents on the left mudguard. Originally coloured pale grey, the dents had been recoloured in a darker shade. The driver's mirror had an almost vertical crack across it.

'Was the driver a Maharashtrian?'

No, she said. He was from the north, most probably from Bihar—or Jharkhand.'

'Not from Bangladesh?'

No, she said, people from Bangladesh have a different accent. Moreover, he had an 'OM' tattooed on his forearm.

'Hmm. What else do you remember about him?'

He was in his late twenties, she said, thin, and about an inch taller than her. His left ear was pierced. His fingernails—a well as toenails—needed to be trimmed. He was dressed in a checked, brown bush shirt over a dark brown pair of trousers and black Kolhapuri chappals a size too large for him. He spoke with a somewhat nasal voice.

In the end she wrote down her husband's mobile number below her signature in the FIR. Her own mobile, she said, was in the purse.

~

The SP's telephone call came one morning a week later. It had been the most dismal week of her life.

'We have received a purse that matches the description you gave us,' he said.

She rushed to the police station.

'The auto driver noticed the purse fifteen minutes or so after you had left the auto,' the SP told her. 'He was at

Churchgate by then but he took a U-turn, went to Bombay Hospital and looked for you there. He could not locate you through your mobile because it was locked.'

'I keep it locked,' she murmured.

'Finally he left the purse at the hospital, thinking that you would approach them. It took the hospital people some days to send it to us.' The SP rang a bell. A havaldar came in with the purse. 'I am sure that it is yours,' the SP continued, 'but you will have to tell us something about its contents before we can hand it over to you. Rules.'

She told him: the side pocket held a pair of earrings and her mangalsutra, with one of its strings frayed and therefore needing repair. The main pocket of the purse contained her mobile, pink in colour; a ring of keys holding three keys, one of them Godrej; a State Bank of India FD for a sum of Rs 3,000; a letter from Bombay Hospital calling her for the interview; her BA and MA certificates; a character certificate from the rector of the university; another certificate from her hockey coach...

'Hockey? You play hockey?'

'I used to. I played for my college.'

'What position?'

'Striker. Left wing.'

'Are you left-handed?' he asked.

'Mostly. I prefer to write with my right hand though.'

'I too used to play hockey...but that was a long time back.' He gave a rueful smile. 'But I have interrupted you. Please continue.'

She continued: her university ID card; her library card; a small address book; a small notebook; a ballpoint pen;

a hairbrush; a pale brown lipstick; a safety pin; a rubber band; a white handkerchief embroidered with a red rose; one 100-rupee note; three 50-rupee notes; four 20-rupee notes; one 10-rupee note; three one-rupee coins; and one 50-paise coin.

'Anything else?'

A frown appeared on her forehead and she closed her eyes. A moment later she opened the eyes and shook her head, 'No. Nothing else.'

'Are you sure?'

'Yes.'

He gave the havaldar by his side a questioning glance. The havaldar, who had been matching her list with a list in the police register, nodded.

'May I have my purse now?' she asked.

'One minute.' The SP rose from the chair and stepped out of the room. A few moments later her sharp ears picked up his voice. He was talking to somebody on the telephone—about her! 'Every single item in the purse, sir, starting with a golden mangalsutra, down to a 50-paise coin... Yes, sir... Also the description of the auto and the driver... Almost as if she knew him... Most unusual, sir.'

She started. Had she said something wrong to the police officer? Desperately, she tried to go over everything she had said to him. But the man was still talking about her!

'The certificates are all there—in the original... She was going for some interview, sir...twenty-three years old, therefore just right... Tall; at least 165 cms... Definitely fit; plays hockey... Yes, married... Yes, sir. Just the type that we are looking for. Moreover, she can use both her hands, so can fire from both hands, ha ha...'

She panicked. Something *had* gone wrong. They had mistaken her for someone else, some criminal… She could not hear him for a few moments. Then she heard him again.

'I was also thinking the same, sir… Yes, sir… Next Tuesday, sir… You can leave that to me, sir… Thank you, sir… No, I will not let her slip out of our hands.'

Before she could think further, he entered the room and took his chair.

She looked up slowly and murmured, 'My purse…'

A smile appeared on his face. 'First, I have to ask you something?

She waited.

'Would you like to join the police?' he asked.

'What!'

'Would you care to join the police?' he repeated. 'As a sub-inspector,' he added.

'I… I…' She searched for words. 'Are you serious?'

He nodded. 'We are having a special recruitment this month,' he said. 'The salary of a sub-inspector is not much, I know,' he continued, 'but you will get a place to live in. And a jeep when on duty. *And* opportunity to play hockey!'

'I…' She fought back the tears that had suddenly risen to her eyes.

'And the promotion prospects are not bad. In my days…' He shrugged his shoulders.

She found her voice. 'I don't know what to say.'

'Say yes,' he said.

'All right,' she said. 'Yes.'

'Thank you. You will have to fill in an application form

and appear for an interview—a formality in your case—next week, Tuesday morning. Come at nine. No, make it eight-thirty.'

'Thank you. I will.'

'You may say "I will, *sir*",' he said with a twinkle in his eyes.

'Thank you, *sir*,' she said with a smile of her own, and saluted him the way she had seen police officers salute their superiors in Hindi films.

Grandmother's Favourite

Azma and I have known each other since we were this high. We are not just first cousins but were also neighbours in Nagpada all through school and college. She was the arty type, and so went to the JJ School of Arts after high school. I studied at Siddharth, the best college in Mumbai for Mass Communication. As JJ was on my way to college, I often gave her a lift on my motorbike. She would sit as far behind me as possible, her hair suitably covered, till we were out of Nagpada. Then she would remove the scarf from her hair, slide close and cling to me all the way to JJ. We were in love years before nani (our grandmother) decided whom Azma should marry.

Azma was nani's favourite. Of course, whenever anyone asked her who of her seventeen grandchildren she loved the most, she always said that she loved all of us equally. But everybody knew it was Azma. I was a close second, I think. She cooked biryani for the whole family—a rare treat—when I got my first job (with *Midday News*) and again when, after I had worked for a year as a stringer for the *New York Times* in Mumbai, got my green card for America.

'Leave the leg for Aslam,' she admonished Maqbool

in front of everybody when she saw him digging into the degchi for a drumstick at my farewell party. 'He likes legs.'

'Actually, I like breasts too,' I said, seizing the drumstick from Maqbool's hand and giving Azma a quick wink.

Azma arranged her dupatta hurriedly and looked round guiltily.

'He is going to Umrika,' nani continued. 'God knows if they have biryani there.'

'They don't,' I said, 'not like yours.'

'I'll make biryani with my own hands the day you and Azma get married,' she said. 'Yes, I've decided,' she continued, addressing the gathering, 'Azma is marrying Aslam.'

For a moment everybody looked stunned. Then they applauded. My mother stepped forward, cracked her knuckles near her own ears, and kissed Azma on her head. Someone gave me a hug. Someone slapped me on the back. Hard. I whirled back. Was it Maqbool? I couldn't be sure. It could be Tariq. Both of them pretended to be listening attentively to nani.

'They will get married in the last week of Rajab,' she concluded.

'Come back for it a week earlier,' she added, this to me.

~

Our wedding six months later was a grand affair, followed by a banquet for almost two hundred guests. There must have been a dozen dishes at the banquet, but everybody made a beeline for nani's biryani, her tastiest ever, and later, the seviyan, also cooked by her with her own hands.

Tears brimmed in her eyes when, at the end of the day, Azma gave her a farewell hug and left with me for my flat—ten yards from her flat, where nani lived.

The next morning, however, when Ammi, Shaukat, Azma and I were sitting round the dining room table, waiting for Fauzia to bring us tea, nani charged into the kitchen, sat down in the chair quickly vacated by Shaukat, drew it close to me and asked me point-blank, right in front of the others, 'Tell me. Do you drink?'

Now nani is not a particularly devout Muslim. For instance, she has never worn a burqa, never even covered her hair. On the contrary, she flaunts it, though it is completely white. Daily she spends almost half an hour before the long mirror in her room, combing her hair and humming songs that nobody else in the family would be caught dead humming. I teased her about her vanity once—I must have been seventeen or eighteen then. She was sitting up in bed against a mountain of pillows, having just recovered from an attack of flu, but still suffering from all sorts of aches and pains that seemed to be taking forever to go.

'Nani,' I said, keeping a straight face, 'if a farishta were to come down from heaven and promise to make you completely well but on condition that you lose your beauty, would you agree?'

She frowned. Everybody waited.

'No,' she said at last. 'All these problems will go away someday.'

Everybody burst out laughing. She sulked the whole day and refused to accept my sorry. She also did not eat anything, saying she was not hungry—till Azma, back from school, and with no idea of what had happened, said out of the blue that she wished she had hair like hers, so long and silky.

Oh yes, she never covered her hair. She was no better with the other dos and don'ts of life either. She never used the word inshallah to give a spiritual flavour to her sentences. She prayed only once a day, that too hurriedly, as if it was something she had to get out of her way, so that she could attend to her real duties, which were to tell her four daughters and three daughters-in-law how to run their homes. As for keeping fasts during the holy month, she fasted only on one or two days, though she made so much fuss over it that the whole mohalla knew of it weeks in advance. And she never went on Haj, though Rafiqmama, her eldest son, who visited Mecca like other people visit the Juhu beach, constantly pestered her to accompany him at least once. No, she was not a devout Muslim. But she drew the line at drinking.

'So answer me, Aslam,' she raised her voice, 'do you drink?' I did not drink much, just a martini or two at lunchtime, a whisky or two before dinner, sometimes a glass of wine with dinner, and finally a small nightcap, mostly a brandy. That was the minimum expected of a budding reporter in New York, that too with the *NYT*. But, of course, it was pointless to try and explain any of this to nani.

'Who says I drink?' I cried.

'Never mind who,' she snapped. 'Answer my question.'

'It must be Maqbool, that swine,' I said.

It did not help. Nani repeated, 'So do you drink?'

'Or is it Tariq?' I asked.

To my astonishment the next sentence came from Azma.

'Answer nani,' she said.

Nani gave her an approving glance and turned back to me.

'So?'

I changed tack. 'What do you think, nani?' I asked. 'Do *you* think I drink?'

'I... People who drink have shining faces,' she said uncertainly.

'And do I have a shining face?' I asked, challengingly enough but making a mental note to check my face when I was before a mirror next.

'I can't make up my mind,' she said. 'That's why I'm asking you.'

I looked around. Everybody was looking at me with troubled eyes, waiting for my reply. I took a deep breath and lied. 'Of course I don't.'

'Hmm...' She stared at me for a long time before speaking again. 'Promise me you will never drink again,' she said.

'What do you mean *again*?' I protested. 'I *said* I don't drink.'

'Promise me,' she cried, loudly this time.

'Oh, I promise,' I muttered.

She stared at me for a longer time now. Then, turning to Azma, she said, 'Please make sure that he does not drink in future.'

'Oh come on, nani,' I cried. 'Don't you trust me?'

'Yes,' she said, looking me up and down peculiarly. Then she turned to Azma and said, 'Trust; but verify.'

Azma nodded her head, slowly but surely. I had to pinch myself when I saw that. Was it the same girl who, just two hours back, was murmuring in my ear that she loved me? What was it about nani, I wondered, that made people do what she wanted them to do? I hoped New York, ten time zones away, would break her spell.

~

But almost the first thing that Azma did when we reached New York, after staring in disbelief at the bottles on a sideboard in my—now her—kitchen, was to purse her lips, roll up her sleeves and pour all the drinks into the kitchen sink, even my rare, double malt Glenfiddich. I opened my mouth to say that the drinks were not for me but for visitors to the house, but one look at her face and I kept quiet. She was never going to be open to reason, not where drinks were concerned. I would just have to factor that in while trying to find a way to drink.

The martinis at lunchtime were not a problem. How to drink after returning home was the problem. Oh, there were plenty of places in our house—we had rented a place in Queen's—where one could safely hide a bottle, the attic for instance, which Azma rarely visited. It would take me only a minute and forty seconds—I timed it—to make a dash to the attic, take a swig or two from the bottle and return to the drawing-dining room. The problem was Azma's nose. She could smell whisky, or gin, or beer, or whatever, from a mile, let alone from my mouth, as she did one evening, when, unable to control myself, I did make that dash to the attic. She did not let me get anywhere near her that night, in fact for a whole week after that.

Then one day Mike—he and I shared a room at office—told me that there was a drink that did not smell: vodka. It also looked like water, he said, truly a great invention. I tried it out at dinner that evening. He was right. Azma did not suspect a thing. I risked it the next evening. Azma still did not suspect a thing. I had found the answer to my problem.

But, as the wise say, every answer in life comes with its own problem. I realized that when, at the dinner table a week later, Azma reached out for my glass of 'water' because she had finished hers and did not want to get up from the table to fetch some more from the fridge. I saved myself by gulping down my drink, begging her pardon with 'I'm sorry, I didn't hear you', fetching from the fridge a bottle of water and pouring some in her—as well as my—glass. That night, however, I went over my strategy again. Clearly I had to fine-tune it, perhaps by mixing the vodka with some drink. Pepsi? No, I decided after a moment's reflection. Azma liked Pepsi. I also rejected Coke, Sprite, tonic water, club soda and orange juice for the same reason. I had to find a drink that she would not pick up, something she did not care for, in fact disliked. Was there any such drink? Yes, I remembered. Tomato juice! She detested it. Actually I too did not much care for it. But the next day I brought home a half litre jar of tomato juice before Azma was due to return from an interview for a job, emptied it in a large jug, poured in it just the right amount of vodka and shoved the jug into the back of the bottom shelf of the refrigerator. It tasted fine at dinner, cool and refreshing. On a whim I added a little salt to it, stirred it well, and took a sip. It tasted better.

Azma raised an eyebrow when she saw what I was drinking.

I tried to deflect her. 'So what happened at the interview?'

'They have offered me a job, that of secretary to their vice president, not the job I wanted, but I've decided to take it—till a better one comes along. I start on Monday.'

'Cheers to that!' I raised my glass.

That was a mistake, I quickly realized, and braced myself for her question.

'Why the tomato juice?' she asked. 'I thought you did not like it.'

'I read somewhere that it increases the zest of a married man's performance,' I said with a smirk. She made a face and said, 'Drink something that decreases it.'

She did not mean it, I knew. It was just the nani in her that had spoken. Actually, she rarely said no to me in bed.

I told Mike about the tomato juice the next day, not the entire story, just the first part of it.

'Add some lemon juice to the mix,' he said, 'along with a dash of Worcestershire sauce, a drop of Tabasco, a pinch of crushed black pepper, and, of course, the salt, and you will be drinking one of the greatest cocktails on earth, Bloody Mary.'

I tried it out that evening. It was great.

Two or three months passed. I altered the amounts of the ingredients, till came the day when Mike said—after tasting a sample I had taken to office for him—that mine was without doubt the best Bloody Mary in all New York. 'You'll have no problem finding another job,' he said, 'if the *NYT* ever fires you.'

I laughed. There was no danger of the paper firing me; they had just raised my salary. Then Azma got herself another job, of making illustrations for an advertising firm, just what she wanted. Our cup of joy could not have got any fuller.

~

Then, when I was sure that we were going to live happily ever after, I got a telephone call from my father in Mumbai. He said that nani had a feeling that she was not going to live much longer. Before dying, she wanted to go on Haj. On the way to Haj, she wanted to visit Azma. She was leaving Mumbai for New York on Sunday, two days hence.

My first thought was of her biryani. I almost said it would be great to have her. Then came the second, sobering thought—of the tomato juice in the fridge!

'New York is not on the way to Mecca,' I said.

'It is, for her,' abba said dryly.

'And Haj is still a month away,' I said.

'Yes,' abba said. 'She wants to visit Azma for a month.'

'She will need visas to come to America,' I remembered.

'She got the visas this morning,' he said.

'You never told me she had applied for the visas,' I cried.

'I wanted to. She said she wanted to give you a surprise.'

'Well,' I pointed out, 'it is no longer a surprise.'

'She thinks it is. She doesn't know about this call.'

'So what should I tell her when she sees me at the airport?' I said sarcastically.

'Say, "What a surprise!"' abba said.

Azma was delighted with the news. She did up the guest room. She got permission from her boss to work from home three afternoons a week. She hired a part-time maid, Manuella, to help with housework and keep nani company for a few hours every morning. She bought a 500-piece jigsaw puzzle for nani to tackle whenever she was by herself. She stocked up the fridge with things she knew nani would like, mostly soft things like cheeses, cakes, yogurts, avocados, strawberries…

'I say, Aslam, do you have to keep your tomato juice in the fridge?' she asked me when she noticed the jug.

'It has to be kept cool,' I said, 'for it to, ahem, work.' She made a face but left the jug alone.

'And who knows, nani may like it,' I added with a straight face, 'not that it has any effect on…'

'She hates tomato juice,' Azma cut me short.

'A pity, that,' I said, hoping my face did not show what I really wanted to say: hallelujah.

~

The subject came up the very first evening after nani came, when she saw me pouring out the tomato juice in my glass.

'Since when have you started drinking *that*?' she cried. 'And why?'

'Tomato juice helps a man to, er…develop his faculties,' I said, enjoying the look of sudden alarm on Azma's face.

'What faculties?' nani asked.

'Mental faculties,' I said. 'One thinks clearer and better after drinking even one glass of it. And in my job,' I added, 'I have to think clearly all the time. Want to try some?'

She gave me a withering look and took a glass of Pepsi that Azma had miraculously poured out and rushed to her side in a second.

~

We gave her the time of her life in the month she spent with us, taking her to restaurants, shopping malls, sightseeing trips in and outside New York…and chatting with her for hours about everything and everybody back home. Manuella took over when we were away at work. She knew no Urdu and nani no Spanish, but right from the start they got along like a house on fire, chatting away in the time-tested lingua franca of the world, signs and laughter. It helped, I suppose, that Manuella was also a grandmother, armed with photographs of all of her nine grandchildren in all sorts of moods, and prepared to bow to nani's score of seventeen. She was also warm-hearted, hard-working and, to nani's satisfaction, no better than her at the jigsaw puzzle, which was slowly spreading out on the coffee table in the drawing room.

I too tried to help her with the puzzle a few times, while waiting for Azma to get the dinner ready, I sipping my tomato juice, nani her Pepsi. The puzzle was not easy, for the scene was something out of a tropical forest, mostly foliage, all in shades of the same colour, green. Even with Manuella's and my help, the puzzle was not even half done after two weeks. 'I must finish it before I go,' nani started to say. 'Help me find the piece for this space, Aslam, and I'll do the rest.'

It was around that time, when nani and I were rummaging through the jigsaw pieces, and laughing happily over some story that I had brought home from office, that I suddenly realized that Azma was beginning to feel miffed about the bonhomie that had developed between nani and me. She knew that she had always been nani's favourite, ever since she was a baby. And lo and behold, nani was treating me as almost her equal. Nani even said to Azma one evening, when Azma was doling out biryani in three plates, 'Give Aslam the leg! He likes legs.' The result? Azma doubled her efforts to please nani. And I? I trebled my efforts. If Azma bought her a scarf, I asked her to by all means wear it, but to never cover her hair with it, for verily, her hair was lovely. I also brought her a 'chocolate panache' that Mike swore his grandmother could not do without for a day—including the day she died. If Azma cooked pasta for her on Friday, I took both of them to a fabulous Italian restaurant near my office on Saturday, and bribed a young and handsome waiter there to insist on seeing an ID proof of nani's age before giving her senior citizen discount (for people over sixty). And when nani laughed and said to the waiter that she was already eighty-two years old and could die any day, I advised her not to be in a hurry, because nana, her husband, was right there in heaven, waiting to question her about all the things she had been doing without him. That brought a sudden look of alarm on her face but she broke into another peel of laughter after that.

'I don't like such talk,' Azma said disapprovingly after the waiter had taken our order and left us.

'What talk?'

'Of people dying.'

'We were just joking,' nani said.

'Yes. *Nani and I* were just joking,' I rubbed in the salt.

'It is a sin to talk of people dying,' Azma persisted.

'Well, nani is going for Haj in three days,' I reminded her. 'That will wipe away all her sins.' Nani loved that.

~

Nani finished the jigsaw puzzle the evening before her departure for Haj. Manuella left us two days later. Azma asked her to continue with us. I too asked her to. I knew that she had been drinking my 'tomato juice' on the sly. For one, the juice level in the jug was often lower than I was sure I had left it. I had also caught her with the jug in her hand one day (though, admittedly, not actually drinking the juice). But what the hell, I had said to myself, if it made her happy, let her drink it. We are not in this world to decide what other people should drink or not drink. So I too asked her to stay on. She smiled, shook her head and said that she was leaving because there was no work for her to do in the house now. I was sure that she was leaving because she found the house sad without nani in it. We too missed nani.

'We must ask her to come again next year,' I said to Azma.

'*You* ask her,' she said tartly. '*You* are her favourite.'

~

Nani spent four days in Mecca, along with Rafiqmama and several other people from Mumbai, and returned to Mumbai at the end of the week. The next day my father telephoned me to convey that she had reached safely. Azma picked up the extension in the kitchen.

'She seems to have had a wonderful time with you,' he said. 'She is full of things she saw and did in New York.'

'What did she enjoy the most, abba?' Azma asked.

'The most?'

'Yes, the most,' she repeated.

'I think, er...some Italian restaurant near Aslam's office,' he said.

'What about things at home?' I asked hurriedly. I did not like the sudden intake of breath I could hear from Azma's extension. 'At home?' he asked, sounding puzzled.

'Yes, what did she like the most of the things she ate at home?'

'Er... She spoke about something called panache,' he said. 'What on earth is panache?'

'Just something made of chocolate,' I hastened to change the subject again. 'What else did she like?' I asked, desperately hoping that he would now say something that would please Azma.

'Oh, I quite forgot,' he said. 'The thing she liked most about the visit was your tomato juice. Absolutely. She tried out every brand of tomato juice available in Mecca. None of them tasted like yours. What brand is it, Aslam?... Aslam?... Hello?... Hello?...'

Women Can't Play It

To tell the truth, I have not thought of her often in recent years, or of him, or of the time we worked together in the Ministry of External Affairs in Delhi. Thirty years is a long time. But when I read in the papers that she had become Foreign Secretary, a hundred memories of those days came back to me in a rush. For a moment I even forgot that I was no longer in Delhi, or even in the Foreign Service for that matter, having retired and settled down in distant Pune.

She was a couple of years junior to me, so about twenty-seven years of age, but we were both of the same rank at that time, under secretaries, in the same division too, Administrative Reforms. We also shared a room. Only deputy secretaries and above were entitled to rooms of their own in those days.

But I see that I am running ahead of the story. In the beginning, there were just he and I. He was Joint Secretary (AR), so the head of the division. Everybody called him Raja saheb, probably because he came from a princely family in Rajasthan, and had been a cricket player of note in his youth. He was also tall. But he drooped a little, so that he looked a little older than his age, which could not have been more than forty-five or six. His eyebrows drooped too, giving his face a melancholy look. Rumour had it that his face was not always so, that it had turned melancholy after his wife left him for another man, a holy man at that. The rumour also said that the man must have mesmerized her, for otherwise who would leave a husband like Raja saheb, an officer and a gentleman. The truth, I now realize, was simpler. Raja saheb was our ambassador in Baghdad at that time. His wife had stayed behind in Delhi to write a book on Hindu Mysticism. And they had no children or close relatives in Delhi. If it had not been that holy man, it would have been some other holy man.

It is not known how Raja saheb took the blow—he tended to keep his feelings to himself—but, according to the rumour, he stopped smiling that day, and his face, long to begin with, acquired the melancholy look. The face came alive whenever he spoke about administrative reforms. 'India can never become great without a first-rate Foreign Service,' he liked to say. 'But to make the Service first-rate, we need to carry out a thousand reforms. Everything, starting with our system of selecting officers, to the method of training them, to improving their conditions of service, to judging their performance…everything needs to be overhauled. The British left behind a mess,' he would continue warmly, 'and the fellows in Finance have only made it worse since we became independent. They say no to everything.'

The fellows in Finance hated him. 'He is taking bread away from our mouths,' they grumbled in unguarded moments. What they meant was that the reforms he got them to approve, invariably after long battles, made it that much more difficult for them to visit London, Paris, Las Vegas and such other places at public expense. 'One doesn't have to go round the world,' he liked to say, 'to take sensible decisions.'

He himself never went abroad on a jaunt. In fact he never went to any place in India either—except on two occasions, both at his own expense, and both to donate blood to strangers who needed it. (He had an extremely rare type of blood called 'Bombay A Positive'.) He spent his days in Delhi, fighting Finance. It was not just with words that he fought them. He did so with action too. Once he applied for a 'vehicle loan' from Finance and bought, of all things, a bicycle with the money, just to tell the world how ridiculously small the amount was. For many weeks he even rode the bicycle to the Ministry every morning from his flat in Moti Bagh, keeping to the middle of the road, causing mini traffic jams everywhere, and finally forcing Finance to make the loan sensible.

He was eccentric all right—and outspoken. In fact it was this habit of his, of shooting straight from the shoulder, that was the cause of his being recalled from Baghdad and posted in Administrative Reforms, which was where the Ministry often sent hot-headed officers to cool down. There was not much work in AR. It consisted almost entirely of requesting Finance to oblige individual officers wanting special favours, exceptions to rules. None of Raja saheb's predecessors had ever asked Finance to actually change a rule. Everybody knew that it would never agree to that; and it was far too fatiguing to fight it. As under secretary in the division, I too had done nothing, nothing really, in the few months I had been working under another Joint Secretary before Raja saheb took over the division. I was the only under secretary in the division at the time. The post of the second under secretary was lying vacant. Wags said that the division already had one under secretary too many.

Raja saheb, however, was not the sort to sit idly in office. The morning he took charge of the division, he just rolled up his sleeves and asked me to bring him all the files. And, well, I dusted the files and took them to his room. Over the next seven days, Sunday included, he went through the files, coming to office at eight in the morning, living on biscuits and tea the whole day, and leaving office at nine at night. I too kept the same hours. There was no one waiting at home for either of us. Moreover, working with him was exciting.

'When you see the same problem recurring again and again,' he said, 'you are looking at a rule that needs to be changed. All that you need to do then is to decide how best to change the rule, and find the right arguments to convince other people to agree with you.' At the end of the week, he rolled up his sleeves again and sent to Finance his first proposal. I still remember what it was. There was a rule that said that an officer going to Colombo on a posting must travel by train and bus up to Kanyakumari, the southern tip of India, and from there by boat. He got the rule changed by proving to Finance that it was cheaper to fly the officer straight from Delhi to Colombo. Before two more weeks were out, he had got Finance to approve half a dozen more reforms. The reforms were minor—they caused no ripples—but they were reforms nevertheless.

Then he picked up a major reform, the Medical Scheme for people posted in our embassies abroad. Three senior Indian diplomats had died in office in the preceding month or so for lack of adequate medical care. Their deaths had come as a shock to us—not only because they were colleagues, but because we discovered that we had no spare officers to fill the vacancies. Our Service was absurdly small, with only about four hundred officers in all, nowhere near enough to handle our greatly expanded responsibilities at home and abroad.

'Moreover too many of our officers are women,' Raja saheb said to me at one point, pausing from a scrutiny of the list of IFS officers, and suddenly asked, 'Do you play chess?'

'Chess?'

'Yes, chess.'

'I used to play it,' I said.

'Well, diplomacy is like a three-dimensional chess game. You have to plan several moves ahead. Women can't do it.'

I had never worked with a woman colleague till then, so had no views on the matter, but I nodded in a non-committal sort of way.

'It is not like sitting at a reception desk,' he continued, 'or writing books.'

I nodded again, but it occurred to me that maybe he was thinking of his wife. I had heard that she was a receptionist at the JN Library when he first met her. And of course she wrote books.

'Anyway,' he said, 'our immediate task is to improve the medical facilities. We can't afford to lose any more men.'

The deaths became both his reason as well as weapon to demand that the rules be changed. Finance argued that the diplomats must have ruined their health by 'too much wining and dining'. He sent to Finance documents showing that two of the senior officers who had died had never touched alcohol, nor meat; the third had passed away in the ICU of a cheap Cairo hospital that was notorious for spreading infection, but was on Finance's small list of 'approved hospitals'. The ding-dong with Finance went on for months till luckily (so to speak) one more senior Indian diplomat abroad died in an 'approved' hospital. Two weeks later, to the astonishment and delight of the whole Service, Finance approved our new Medical Scheme. Overnight, Raja saheb became a hero.

More changes followed—in the rules governing children's education, computation of daily allowances, payment of emoluments in convertible currency, renting of houses… We had carried out almost a hundred reforms, big and small, before one more year was out. But I was still the only under secretary in the division. The other desk in my room was still unoccupied. Under secretaries—all grades of officers—were in short supply. And none of the few under secretaries that were available every now and then wanted to work in AR division. All of them wanted glamorous, high-profile assignments.

~

Suddenly one morning, there was a knock on Raja saheb's door—we were at our daily morning meeting—and *she* entered the room. He was telling me how to frame our proposal on cadre review; Finance had already shot it down once; but the Service desperately needed more officers; we had to find a way to persuade Finance to approve the review, which alone would help us recruit more officers. He stopped and looked at her over the rim of his glasses. Sitting across his table, I too looked back.

'I am Indira Iyengar, Under Secretary,' she said from the door. 'May I come in, sir?'

He nodded.

She walked in slowly, and stood behind a chair to my right. She was fair for a Tamil, and endowed with a slim waist but ample hips that many women from the south have. She also had their large, dark and somewhat mysterious eyes. 'I have just returned from Brussels, sir,' she said. 'I was Second Secretary in our embassy there.' She had a soft voice.

'Y-es?' he said, and waited. I too wondered what she had come for. Probably for some special favour, exception to some rule, in which case she had come at a wrong time. Raja saheb hated to be interrupted at our morning sessions.

What she said took my breath away. 'I want to work under you sir,' she said, 'in AR division.'

'Hmm,' he said, removing his spectacles and beginning to wipe them. My heart sank. I knew what the gesture meant; he was going to say no. Should I say something to change his mind? We desperately needed an extra pair of hands.

She spoke before I could make up my mind. 'You are a Rajput, sir,' she said to Raja saheb. 'I'm sure that you won't say no to a request from a wo…from me.'

If there was one word that stopped Raja saheb in his tracks, it was this, Rajput, with its shades of chivalry, gallantry, generosity, hospitality, valour, pride, self-sacrifice... He smoothened his moustache with the side of a crooked forefinger, then cleared his throat and asked her to sit down.

She curled back a strand of hair that had escaped from her plait—the plait reached her waist—and sat down.

'Would you care for some tea? Or would you prefer coffee?' he asked.

'May I have a soda, Raja saheb, club soda?'

He ordered a club soda for her and tea for the two of us. Then he asked someone on the intercom to issue orders posting her in AR division, and turned to us, 'Basically, AR work consists of identifying recurring problems in management of men and material, and finding sensible solutions for them...' His briefing lasted ten minutes.

'Joshi?' he said in the end, addressing me.

'Yes, Raja saheb?'

'Divide the work. I suggest that henceforth you should handle only the proposals that are already in the pipeline. Let Indira handle the new proposals, the ones we have yet to send to Finance. Help her with them till she settles down.'

'Yes, Raja saheb,' I said happily, delighted to have someone to share the work with.

'And bring her with you for our morning meetings from tomorrow.'

I escorted her to my room—now *our* room—showed her her desk, and asked my peon—now *our* peon—to bring out all the files from the three almirahs in the room. 'Believe me,' I said with a laugh as the peon brought out bundles of files, 'we have miles to go before we sleep… Raja saheb is a visionary. He wants to make our Foreign Service the best in the world.' And I separated the files into hers and mine.

In the weeks that followed, however, I discovered four things, all of them dismaying.

First, I was getting drawn to her. And I had no business to let that happen. I was engaged to a girl from a good family in Kolhapur that my parents had selected for me. The wedding date had also been fixed, some six months away.

Second, Indira had no interest in reforms, and certainly no aptitude for it. I rarely saw her buried in a file. If she was buried in anything at all, it was in her telephone, chatting away in Tamil with God knew who all. I ended up doing almost all of her work.

Third, as a result, my own work was suffering; and the overall output of the division was actually beginning to decline. The rationalization of allowances had gone into hibernation; so also the increase in servants' wages, hardship station allowances, purchase of chanceries abroad… The most dismaying of these was, of course, the cadre review. She just could not—or would not—come to grips with it, no matter how hard I tried to explain it to her.

And fourth, I did not know how to stop spending most of my time on her work. Somehow, it was impossible to say no to her. Worse, I had to watch Raja saheb openly admiring her work—in truth, my work—at our morning meetings. I still recall the mounting excitement with which he read her (i.e. my) proposal on how to get Finance to sanction the strengthening of our embassies in the Gulf. 'An excellent plan,' he said, patting the file after he had finished reading her (i.e. my) note, 'reducing posts in our High Commission in London—which is bloated with auditors and accountants and purchase officers, all useless people—and strengthening our embassies in the Gulf with the money thus saved. I can't see how Finance can say no to the proposal. Excellent! Excellent!'

Did she say that it was my draft, like almost all the other proposals of hers? Not on your life. She just gave him a grateful smile.

A few days later, when again he praised 'her' work, she said to him that he was her source of inspiration. A few further days later she said that he was truly a visionary; he wanted the Indian Foreign Service to become the best in the world… Came a day when she stayed back in his room after the morning session. 'I need to consult him about one or two things,' she said without bothering to tell me what things. That happened again, and again. Some days I actually felt like a kebab-mein-haddi, a thorn between two roses… And one day all of a sudden I realized what she was up to. She was trying to seduce him. Yes, however improbable the thing seemed—a girl her age trying to seduce a divorced man almost twenty years older than her—there was no other explanation for her conduct. As to why she was doing that, it was not difficult to guess. He was almost a celebrity, wealthy too, so a great catch for a husband. Was he getting seduced? Yes, he was, I concluded after studying him for a few days at our morning meetings.

What was more, I was falling in love with the girl myself—with her eyes, her smile, her long, smooth neck, her walk, her talk... I came alive when she entered the room every morning. I died when, come five o'clock, she left the room. And I absolutely hated the weekend, for that kept me away from her for two whole days.

~

Then one day she did not come to office. She telephoned to ask me to tell Raja saheb that she would not be able to attend the morning meeting.

'What reason should I give him, in case he asks?'

'Tell him...tell him...that I am not well,' she said.

Something in her voice told me that that was really the reason.

'Is anything the matter, Indira?' I asked. I could hear voices behind her. 'Where are you?'

'I'm all right,' she said. 'It is just that... We will talk later.'

I covered up for her, telling Raja saheb that she was not well, but with a hint that women are often unwell, so it was not something to worry about... In a way her absence turned out to be a blessing. I could discuss a lot of my own files with Raja saheb that morning. But I missed her.

When she came to office, well after lunch, she behaved normally. But her fingers gave her away. They kept drumming her desk, and she hardly looked at the files on her desk. She did not tell me what was troubling her, and I did not press her. Surprisingly, she made no telephone calls either.

A fortnight later, once again she telephoned me to ask me to tell Raja saheb that she was not feeling well and would be coming late to office.

'Where are you?' I cried. This time I was sure she was in some public place.

She kept quiet.

'Where are you, Indira?' I cried again, more insistently this time.

'I am…in hospital?'

'What! Which hospital?'

'The Army Hospital in Dhaula Kuan?'

'What are you doing in the Army Hospital?'

'I am here for…treatment.'

'But you are a civilian.'

'My husband is in the army,' she murmured. The earth shook under me.

'Husband?' I asked when I could speak again. 'You are married? You never told me.'

'I didn't?… He is in Signals. He is posted in Mhow at present.'

'But your surname has not changed,' I said stupidly. 'I know it was Iyengar when you joined the Service.'

'My husband's surname is also Iyengar.'

That stumped me. 'What treatment are you in hospital for?' I asked next.

'Dialysis.'

I was not sure what dialysis was, but it did not sound nice.

I covered up for her at the meeting with Raja saheb that morning. If he felt that anything was amiss, he did not show it, but he did not pay much attention that morning to work either, and asked me to let him know when she came to office. She did not come to office the whole day.

That night, however, when I telephoned her, she talked. It was like a dam bursting. She had been betrothed to her husband when both of them were children. They were cousins. They belonged to a community that allowed marriages between cousins. The community, small in size and therefore tightly-knit, consisted of descendants of a few families from Tanjore that had migrated to Andhra Pradesh in the seventeenth century. Cut off from their larger community in Tamil Nadu, they had evolved their own customs, including that of marrying cousins... She had got married just before she went to Brussels. He had accompanied her to the place, but had to return to Mhow when his leave expired. Otherwise he would not have got his promotion to captain in time. He was trying to get transferred to Delhi now.

'Have you told Raja saheb all this?' I asked.

'Er...not yet. I...don't want him to think that I am asking him for help in transferring my husband to Delhi.'

The reason made no sense to me, and I said so to her.

'I will tell him after my husband gets transferred to Delhi,' she said in reply.

I telephoned a doctor friend of mine to ask him what dialysis was all about. He said that if she required dialysis this frequently, every fortnight, at least one of her kidneys was functioning poorly, perhaps both kidneys. You don't require more than one kidney, he continued; the other is like a spare wheel; but if both are defective, you are in serious trouble.

It was only after I had put down the telephone that I thought of the old question again. What was she up to? And why was she wooing Raja saheb? Since it was clearly not to make a husband out of him, there had to be some other reason. Could it be that she only wanted his help to get posted to some place in the West with good medical facilities, like Washington or New York? In normal circumstances, after Brussels, she would only be sent to an underdeveloped country, most likely in Africa. With Raja saheb's support she could easily get the posting of her choice.

The next morning I asked her whether her dialysis was for one kidney or both of them.

She pretended not to have heard me. I decided not to press her, not then. She was more communicative on the telephone, I had realized… I telephoned her on some pretext that evening and casually repeated my question.

'Both kidneys,' she replied.

'How long will the dialysis continue?'

'It depends on how fast my kidneys get well. I have started taking an Ayurvedic medicine also. I am told it helps.'

The remarkable thing about the days that followed was that she—and I—continued to behave 'normally' in office. I kept doing her work; she kept impressing Raja saheb with her work—and continued wooing him.

One day as I rose after the morning session, she said, not rising with me, 'I have to discuss one or two things with Raja saheb.'

'Sure,' I said, and left them.

As it should happen, I had forgotten to take back one of my files, missed it half an hour later, and returned to Raja saheb's room for it. I knocked at the door before entering it, but they did not hear the knock. I was inside the room before Raja saheb saw me—and hastily withdrew his hand from hers. They were holding hands across the table and staring into each other's eyes! I pretended not to have seen anything, just collected my file, muttering something, and left the room.

Was I surprised by what I had seen? Not really. But I was perplexed. What on earth was she doing, a married woman, suffering from a dangerous ailment, fooling around with a man old enough to be her father?

She stayed back in his room the next morning as well, and the morning after that…

'Have you told Raja saheb about the dialysis?' I asked her a few days later.

She pretended not to have heard me.

I changed tack. 'When do you have to go to hospital again?'

'On Friday…'

But it was on Wednesday that she called from hospital.

'It is Wednesday today,' I said the first thing that came to my head.

'The doctors suggested that I should have the dialysis today. Henceforth, I will need to have it every week,' she added.

That sounded ominous. 'Is anybody with you in hospital?'

'My neighbour. My husband was going to come, but… he did not get leave.'

'Where are your parents?'

'They live in Bangalore. I don't want them to worry. They have three other children to worry about!'

This time I did not cover up for her. I told Raja saheb all about her dialysis. 'By the way, she is married,' I added. 'Her husband, who is a captain in the army, was supposed to come here, but...'

'Her husband is a bit of a bounder, you know,' he interrupted me to say.

'Oh!'

'He flirted with an air hostess in the plane to Brussels.'

'Oh!'

'And carried on with the local interpreter in the embassy,' he continued. 'That too on his honeymoon!... And presently he is having an affair with a married woman in Mhow. That's the real reason he has never come to Delhi during her visits to hospital. Poor girl.'

So she had told him, in fact more than she had told me. It also explained to me the holding of hands in his room. But was that all? No. Something had grown between them, I sensed. I felt sure of it in the days that followed. She spent hours in his room every day.

Again, however, came the day she had to go to hospital and did not come to office.

I telephoned her that evening.

'My kidneys are failing,' she said when I pressed her to tell me. There was panic in her voice. 'The doctors say that I need a new kidney.'

I had read that the Government had passed a law curbing the sale of kidneys, but they were still available in the black market.

'I have a doctor friend who might be able to find one for you,' I told her.

'That won't be easy,' she said. 'You see, my blood is of an extremely rare type. I can take a kidney from only someone with the same type of blood.'

'What type?'

'Bombay A Positive.'

'Oh, Raja saheb's blood is of the same type!' I cried out. She did not say anything.

'Do you know that?' I asked. She kept silent.

So she knew that... And a monstrous thought began to form in my mind. She must have known it from the day it came in the papers—almost a year back—that Raja saheb had travelled all the way to Coimbatore to donate his blood to a stranger... That, in fact, must be her real reason for joining the AR division. She cared a hoot for reforms. She was interested only in worming her way into Raja saheb's heart. No, she was not after his heart. She was after his kidney! Too shocked for words, I said something polite and put down the phone.

I slept fitfully that night. For once, I was also late to office the next morning. The first thing that I did upon reaching it was to go to Raja saheb. I wanted to warn him of what, I was sure, would soon be coming his way.

He spoke before I could. 'Would you believe it?' he began, his voice more cheerful than ever before. 'Indu and I have the same blood type! A most remarkable coincidence. I told her not to worry. Nobody needs two kidneys. I certainly don't! Indu said that...'

He went on talking. All that I could register was the way

his eyes lit up every time he uttered the name Indu. (Till that moment I had no idea that Indu was her pet name.) She did not come to work that day.

I got a call from her the next day though—again from hospital. She had a question to ask me, she said.

'Do you think that people change when they get other people's kidneys?'

'Change in what way?' I asked.

'In any way,' she replied. 'The ancient Greeks believed that the seat of love is not the heart; it is the kidney.'

'Oh!'

'Can you do me a favour?' she continued. 'Can you ask your doctor friend if he knows?'

I checked with my friend. 'To be honest, I have no idea,' he said. 'I doubt if anybody has carried out any research on it. But it is an interesting thought.'

I conveyed the reply to her. She received it in silence, and just said that she would not be coming to office for a few days.

A couple of days passed. The third day I ran into her husband, of all people, when I was about to enter my place—a single room with a kitchenette in the Ministry's hostel on Kasturba Gandhi Marg. He had been waiting for me for almost an hour outside the door.

'I am Captain Iyengar,' he said when he saw me opening the door, 'Indira's husband.'

I said I was pleased to meet him. 'Do come in.'

He did not move. 'Who is this Raja saheb?' he asked instead.

'He…'

'And why does he want to give his kidney to my wife?'

'I...'

'Don't interrupt me! Just tell him that if he is trying to fool around with my wife, I will...I will...'

I placed a gentle hand on his arm. He brushed it away.

'Raja saheb is a very kind man,' I said nevertheless. 'When he learned that he has the same, extremely rare, type of blood as your wife's, and is therefore the only man that can save her, he...'

'What do you mean the only man? I too have Bombay A Positive type blood.'

'Oh!' I swallowed. The next moment an idea came to me. 'Then why don't you give her one of your kidneys?'

He turned silent. I waited.

He found his voice. 'God has not given us two kidneys for nothing,' he said.

'Ah!... God!... His ways are inscrutable. Well, keep your kidneys then. Let Raja saheb give her one of his kidneys. As for what you called fooling around, I know that Raja saheb is a lonely man, but I can assure you that there is nothing between him and her—not yet,' I added after a meaningful pause.

He started. 'What do you mean *not yet*? Do you mean to say that something is going to happen between them in future?'

I turned the screw a bit. 'Well, the seat of love is not the heart, you know. It is the kidney.'

He frowned.

I continued, 'I have no idea what happens when a man gives his kidney to a woman. Perhaps nothing happens. On the other hand...' I shrugged.

He took a deep breath. A moment passed. He looked at me, opened his mouth to say something, but closed it, turned and walked out of the building.

It was much later that night that it occurred to me that it was odd that he was waiting for me outside my place that evening. How did he know that I lived here? How did he even know who I was, or of my connection with Raja saheb? Surely he could only have learnt all of this from…

~

Late next morning she called—from hospital.

'My husband is giving me one of his kidneys.'

'Congratulations,' I said, my voice dripping with sarcasm.

'The doctors are carrying out some tests on him,' she continued. 'If all goes well, the operation will be done tomorrow. Would you please convey this to Raja saheb?'

'Why don't you tell him yourself?'

'I don't know how to. You see, he was most insistent that I take his kidney, and I had kind of promised him that I would.'

'I see. Was it before or after you asked your husband to meet me?'

She did not say anything.

'Before or after?' I repeated.

'It occurred to me suddenly,' she said weakly.

'Like a move in a three-dimensional chess game, right?'

'Eh?'

'Never mind,' I said. 'Best of luck for tomorrow.'

I hated to give Raja saheb her message. He had been

cheerful the whole morning. He turned melancholy after I gave him the message. 'I only wanted Indu to have one of my kidneys,' he murmured at the end, more to himself than to me. 'That would have been…good enough.'

~

Indira never returned to AR. I myself left it a few weeks later to get married, then go abroad. Raja saheb left it a month later. The cadre review remained a wish in our long list of wishes.

Cherchez la Femme

De Gaulle once said that old age is like a shipwreck. If so, my ship is an exception. I am ninety-three years of age and enjoy what can only be called excellent health. My wife, who is eighty-seven, likes to claim credit for it. I let her have her say. There is no mileage in getting into an argument with her.

People often ask me what is the secret of my good health. My answer is always the same. Eat, drink, exercise, do whatever you want to, but do it in moderation. More importantly, cultivate some interests. My interests, apart from playing golf at Delhi Golf Course twice a week—are reading, writing and speaking about international affairs. I should add that I am a retired diplomat. I joined the Indian Foreign Service when I was barely twenty-four, rose to serve as India's ambassador to a number of important countries, became Secretary in the Ministry of External Affairs and, after retiring from the Service, had a seven-year stint as Advisor to the Government. Yes, mine has been a fine record of service to the nation. Even today, people invite me to speak on international affairs.

But there is a pebble in my shoe, a memory of a failure. It goes back decades, to the time when I was First Secretary in the Indian embassy in Iran. Iran was ruled by a king then, Shah Mohammad Reza Pahlavi, better known as the Shah of Iran. The embassy's mandate was to improve our relations with Iran. It was not an easy task, for Iran's foreign policy was tilted in favour of Pakistan—and against India. No matter how hard I tried, no matter how hard everybody in the embassy tried, the tilt remained...

Years passed. The world changed. The monarchy in Iran was overthrown. It became a theocratic nation. Slowly, India's relations with Iran improved. But I never forgot that all my efforts to improve Indo-Iran ties in those early days had been unsuccessful. Why? The thing remained a mystery.

~

One day, shortly after I became Secretary in MEA, the Pakistani High Commissioner to India came to meet me. It was a courtesy call. We chatted about this and that. I told him that my first job in the Service was that of protocol officer; I had enjoyed it. He told me that his first job too was that of a protocol officer. How did you find the job? I asked him. Most interesting, he said. And he went on to tell me an amazing story:

'The Shah of Iran once visited Karachi on a brief visit,' he began.

'The Shah?' I sat up.

'Yes. Unfortunately, the visit came at a most awkward time for us. An Indian cricket team was playing a test match in Karachi the same week. And everybody in the Protocol Division wanted to go for the test, especially on the last, crucial, day. It fell on me, the junior-most officer in the Division, to accompany the Shah everywhere on that day. I took him to a wreath-laying ceremony, a couple of meetings, a press conference, and a luncheon with our Prime Minister. The afternoon had been kept aside for sightseeing and shopping. All of a sudden I got a brainwave. "Would Your Majesty care to see a cricket match instead?" I asked him.

'"What is a cricket match?" he asked.

'I told him, adding that our cricket team would be delighted to see him there, and took him to the stadium. It was almost 4 o'clock by then, with only an hour's play left. But it was a critical moment for the Pakistani team. It had already lost five batsmen. There was only one decent batsman left; the rest of the players were bowlers. And the team still had to make seventy runs. Bookies outside the pavilion had lowered Pakistan's chances of winning the match to 1 in 25.

'The moment the Shah and I entered the VIP box, however, the Pakistani batsman at the crease hit the ball for a six. And the stadium erupted in a crescendo of clapping and whistling. For a moment, the Shah just stood by his sofa chair, looking stunned. Then slowly he raised his hand and waved to the spectators, turning from left to right, and again to the left, before taking his chair. Good God, I said to myself, the fellow had jumped to the conclusion that all that clapping was for him! By and by, he sat down. The play resumed. A few minutes later, the batsman hit the ball for a second six! The clapping was wild this time, with many people rising to their feet. Mercifully, the Shah did not get up. He just waved his hand, but he looked pleased as punch. And thus it went: several boundaries, some sneaky singles, a third six, a couple of overthrows by increasingly nervous Indian fielders, a few wides by Indian bowlers, a missed catch, even a no ball, all the way to the last ball of the last over. The batsman sent it for a four, winning the test with a flourish. Everybody in the stadium jumped up and began to clap, stopping only when the Pakistani batsmen returned to the pavilion—below our box.

'Then I got another brainwave. I requested the Pakistani captain to bring up the team to meet the Shah. The captain was happy to do so. What was more, a couple of the boys even said to the Shah, as they walked up one by one to shake hands with him, "You brought us luck, Your Majesty!" All this when firecrackers were bursting all around the stadium and a huge crowd of spectators was gathering below the box, really to cheer our team but, oh well, the team was in the VIP box with the Shah… Afterwards, an Iranian protocol officer told me that the Shah had never been so warmly welcomed in his whole life, not even the day he was crowned.'

When the Pakistani High Commissioner reached the end of the story, I laughed appropriately and changed the subject. But I knew that my decades-old mystery had been solved—I mean, half solved. I now knew why the Shah was biased in favour of Pakistan. But why, at the same time, did he keep distant from India?

~

For the answer to that, I had to wait some more years. I was Advisor to the Government then and one day a former Director of Bhabha Atomic Research Centre, BARC, came to meet me. We had met once before, at an IAEA meeting in Vienna. I had found him to be a most affable man, humorous, and a fine storyteller.

'What will you have?' I asked him, 'tea, coffee or something cold?'

'Something cold,' he said.

'How about a Coca-Cola?' I asked.

'No!' he cried, his voice suddenly a few decibels higher. I raised an eyebrow.

'No Coca-Cola,' he said, lowering his voice. 'I am allergic to the very word. No, it has nothing to do with our troubles with the Americans over this Nuclear Suppliers Group business. The fact is that the word reminds me of a most embarrassing episode in my life.'

'What episode?'

'The Shah of Iran's visit to BARC.'

I sat up (only the second time in my life). I knew that when the Shah paid a visit to India, Pandit Nehru had included in his programme a tour of our nuclear reactor at BARC in Bombay. The idea was to impress the Shah with our scientific progress. I had not imagined that anything unusual could have happened there. But obviously something had. 'So what happened?' I asked.

He told me the story: 'I was young then, but I still remember every moment of that afternoon. The Shah's programme in BARC consisted, first, of his going round the place with Bhabha and a couple of other senior scientists. At the end of the tour, they were to bring him to the auditorium, where he would address the scientists and others already assembled. I was in charge of the arrangements in the auditorium; the chairs, the mikes, the refreshments... I had asked our embassy in Iran to let me know what the Shah liked to drink: fresh coconut water? Nimbupani? Rooh Afza? The embassy had replied that the Shah liked Coca-Cola, only Coca-Cola. Happily, Coca-Cola was available in Bombay, but not in Trombay, where BARC was located. The entire stretch from Sion to BARC was almost a wilderness in those days. We had to get all our supplies from Sion. So I had got my peon to bring a whole case of Coca-Cola from there the previous evening, twenty-four bottles. Then, closer to the hour of the function, I had got him to bring several blocks of ice from an ice factory in nearby Mankhurd, and put the bottles in a large tub full of ice. It was an unusually warm day and the auditorium was not air conditioned. The Shah was sure to want his Coca-Cola cold. I had also brought to the function several bottles of mineral water and put them in the tub.

'The function began on time. Bhabha and the Shah walked in side by side; everybody stood up; the two climbed the dais and took their chairs; everybody sat down. The Shah reached for the mineral water bottle that I had placed on the coffee table in front of him. I grabbed two bottles of chilled Coca-Cola, two straws and an opener and rushed up. "A Coke, sir?" I asked the Shah.

'The Shah gave me a curious look and said no. "It is chilled, sir," I said.

'He shook his head.

'Crestfallen, I gave Bhabha his bottle and returned to base. Somebody whispered to me that I should not have used the word Coke. One does not use vulgarisms before a king. I should have said Coca-Cola. "Oh," I said.

'Bhabha began his speech. I kept muttering "Coca-Cola" to myself. At the end of Bhabha's speech, a young girl went up the dais and gave the Shah a bouquet of flowers. Next a senior scientist went up and gave him a gift, a Kashmiri shawl. Then I went up with a chilled bottle, straw and opener. "A Coca-Cola, sir?" I asked.

'This time he did not even look at me. He just brushed me away with a no.

'I returned to base once more. Somebody then hissed to me that I should have said "Your Majesty", not "sir". He was a king after all. Sweating by then, I pursed my lips and nodded.

'The Shah now got up, went to the lectern, and made his speech. I hardly heard it. I was thinking of the mistakes that I had made. I got my third chance when the Shah returned to his chair. I wiped the sweat from my brow, went up the dais with a bottle, straw and opener, and said, correctly this time, "Would you care for a Coca-Cola, Your Majesty?"

'This time he looked at me, gave a sort of smile and said, "No. I am quite happy with the water." He showed me the glass of water in his hand.

'Crushed, and wondering what mistake I had made now, I came down the dais as someone went up the steps to make a valedictory speech. All that effort wasted… I nodded listlessly to my PA and let him and others pounce on the Coca-Cola bottles, now swimming in the tub of ice and water.

'The valedictory speech was long, and frankly, awful. I noticed the Shah look impatiently at his watch a couple of times, and sip water till no water came out of the bottle when he lifted it to pour some more in his glass. He frowned. I picked up a fresh chilled bottle of water and waited till the speech was over. Then I rushed up with the bottle. The Shah looked at the bottle, shook his head and said, "I think I will have that Coca-Cola now."

'In panic, I rushed down the dais, hoping that at least one bottle was saved. They had all gone. In their place somebody had put a few bottles made of thick glass and containing variously coloured, variously flavoured, variously sugared, gas-filled drinks topped with marbles. (These ethnic drinks cost one anna a bottle and were available everywhere. Coca-Cola cost four annas.) I picked up three of the bottles and rushed up the dais. I did not need to take the opener with me; one opened the bottle by pushing down the marble with one's thumb. I offered the Shah a yellow-coloured drink. He gave the bottle an unbelieving look and said no. "What about this one, sir—I mean, Your Majesty?" I blabbered, holding up a scarlet one. No, he cried. "This?" I held up the last one, coloured brown. He started, jumped out of his chair and quickly scrambled down the dais, followed by Bhabha…

'I swore that day never to have anything to do with Coca-Cola,' he concluded.

I laughed, and said 'Eureka!' to myself. I had found the reason why the Shah had kept India at arm's length. His foreign policy defied common sense; any day India was better to befriend than Pakistan; but monarchs are also human beings. Being cheered by thousands of Pakistanis in the Karachi cricket stadium was obviously a far happier experience than being offered strangely coloured drinks, one by one, in BARC.

~

That evening itself, however, I had second thoughts. I was dining at the French embassy, and at one point the French ambassador said, '*Cherchez la femme, toujours cherchez la femme.*' He was referring to something that had happened in England, but I reeled. Obviously, my mystery was not yet fully solved. The real reason for the Shah's bias, the proverbial straw that broke the camel's back, must have had something to do with a woman. Maybe he had an Indian nanny that spanked him. Or maybe, after he came of age, he had been spurned by some Indian girl. Or maybe, he had a Pakistani mistress… In the days that followed, I went through a couple of biographies of the Shah. They had nothing to say about any such women in his life. I went through my own diary of my years in Iran, just in case. It had nothing useful to say either. I gave up the search, deciding that I would probably never solve the mystery.

Years kept rolling. I turned eighty, then ninety, then ninety-three. Then came this morning, when two friends of mine and I were about to start a round of golf, and a stranger with an army moustache walked up to us and asked if he could join us. He turned out to be a retired general. He had joined some firm in Dubai after retiring from the army. Now, almost eighty-five years of age, he had returned to Delhi and resumed golf.

We began chatting, like golfers do the world over while walking on fairways. Came a moment when I said that I had visited Dubai a long time back, when I was posted in Iran. And he said that he had visited Iran from Dubai just a month back.

'For any special reason?' I asked.

'No. Just to see it.'

'Why?' I asked him. 'I mean why now? No tourists go to Iran these days, with the clouds of war gathered over it.'

'I always wanted to see that country,' he said, 'ever since the Shah of Iran visited the National Defence Academy in Khadakwasla back in 1955.'

'The Shah?'

'Yes,' he said. 'I was a senior cadet there, therefore privileged to sit at the high table at the glittering banquet in honour of the Shah, along with the Commandant of the Academy, General Habibullah, several other senior officers and, of course, the Shah himself. Hundreds of smartly turned out cadets sat before us at round tables that I could see all the way to the entrance. It was a great honour for me, and without doubt the most memorable part of my entire training period, though most of the talking at the high table was done by General Habibullah and a couple of senior officers. The Shah himself hardly said a word. It was almost as if something was weighing on his mind. At one point, however, he asked General Habibullah why ladies were not allowed at the banquet. The General replied that it was an old tradition, going back to the nineteenth century. The Queen of England was the only lady allowed to attend Defence College banquets.

'Later I learnt that the Shah had not asked the question just to make conversation. There was a reason for his question. He had come to India with his spouse, Queen Soraya. And Queen Soraya, famous for her temper, had thrown an almighty tantrum when told that since she was a lady, she could not attend the banquet. She would have to make do with a small dinner hosted by Begum Habibullah, to which all the senior ladies at the station had been invited. She had not enjoyed the small dinner. And, from what the guard posted outside the royal suite told us the next day, she gave the Shah hell when he returned from the banquet.'

'Well, well, well,' I laughed, and invited the general to the 19th hole, the bar, for a drink after the game.